ROOK

I0719996

BY FRANCIS LACE

Copyright 2023 Francis Lace Publications

All rights reserved. No part of this book may be reproduced or used in any manner without the prior written permission of the copyright owner, except for the use of single-line quotations in a book review with prior approval from the author. No AI software has been used to create this text and no permission is given for its use in AI software.

Cover Illustration by Rhu. Instagram @rhudraws

Dedication

For my husband, despite his best efforts to distract me.

Content Warning

In this book, there are graphic depictions of sexual situations and acts.

This is a polyamorous romance novel therefore there will be characters with multiple partners, of either the same or opposite gender, with whom they are intimate.

Chapter 1

Enchantress

I t's fading. The richness of the world is not what it once was; its lustre has dimmed. The trees are no longer the bright, full blooms they once were and seem to sag, limp with the weight of a sadness I also bear. We mourn together the fellows lost. What once was strong, bountiful and endless has become worn, aged and weak, and I am forced into farewells I had never planned on enduring.

The water that once shone and tasted so sweet seems dull, and where the flow once roared, it is now constricted and passive. I used to feel its happiness, the ringing of its notes as it went forth on its merry journey, connecting me to the rest of the island and those who would revere me. But it is now hesitant, and I feel its heartache within my chest.

From over the mountains, the air used to come fresh and heavy with promises, whereas now it is sullen and inattentive to me. Its taste has become insipid, and no longer fills my lungs.

I reach into the soil to find loneliness. A loneliness that chills my body and, when left unchecked, creates in my mind a never-ending blackness where nothing grows. This isn't right. The natural flow should not create such solitude. Instead, there should be the loving embrace of the kinship around us.

I can't let this happen! My beloved cannot die. We would all be lost.

The love of the few keeps me from falling into despair and holds the darkness at bay, but if it continues fading this way, I will have to tell them. They may have noticed the smallest changes, but the whole picture will not yet be clear to them. It is unclear even to me.

Oh, to see them frolic in the sun and rejoice at the harvest, their cares and worries forgotten. Their innocent pleasure lifts me and gives me hope.

My darlings, sweet darlings that love, care for and sustain me. They dedicate themselves to me, looking to me for sustenance, comfort, and stability. I am the one who provides for them and keeps them through the cold winters.

To disappoint them would break me.

Chapter 2
Rook

On the highest ridge in the Green Mountains, I finally stopped to catch my breath. My bare chest was slick with sweat, my body exhausted. I staggered to my hands and knees. My throat was dry, my legs ached, and my feet sore from the steep climb of uneven rocks I had stumbled over to make it this far. Pausing a moment, head lowered, I watched the sweat drip from my forehead to the ground, darkening the stone for a moment before disappearing. How much more will this journey take?

Years of farm labour had toned my tall frame, but the strength I had gained over the years hadn't prepared me for the climb. I knew it wouldn't be easy, but I hadn't expected it to be that tough. Taking one last deep breath, I pushed myself to my feet, wiping my wet hair off my face as I lifted my head.

It was a bright spring day, a slight chill clinging to the air cooled my skin. The heightening sun would soon burn away the morning dew and shorten the shadows, so I could not linger. Relieved to spot a puddle in the shadow of a large rock, I scurried over to it and dipped my hands into the cool water, splashing it over my head and letting it run through my hair and down my neck and shoulders, enjoying the cool tracks left on my skin. Lowering my face once more, I scooped my hands through the water again to scrub away some of the grime off my face, feeling the scratch of my unshaven jaw. What my mother would say to say to see me so unkept, she would also croon to me of my appearance. My dark hair and muscular physique had brought no end of longing looks from the young women in my home village of Harth. My father had constantly urged me to choose one as a suitable wife, but I had never really been interested in any of them enough to want to commit myself to them with marriage. Many were pretty enough but all were dull. They never wanted to talk about anything of great interest or insight, just the same inane conversations again and again; how best to fix their hair, what unnecessary trinkets they bought on market day, who the tavern girl was bedding.

I had had a short dalliance with the baker's daughter, who had enjoyed sucking my cock in the barn, but it hadn't lasted the year. If she wasn't in the bakery or dragging me into the barn, she was in the tavern, boasting of the farm she would inherit when we married and seeing how many cups of mead she could get through before the sunset. Despite the pleasure her mouth gave me when we were alone, I quickly tired of spending evening after evening waiting for her to fall off the bar so I could carry her home.

My brothers on the other hand, enjoyed the attention of the women in the village, competing to see how many they could bed and letting the number be known to me, despite my insistence that I didn't care. They were handsome men, so most of the women were happy to accept their advances, even though, given their reputation, it was unlikely to last. I had once stumbled across my eldest brother with the serving maid in the alley beside the tavern. His hips were thrusting so hard and fast the girl had to brace herself against the hitching rail, the horses in their stalls looking on with mild curiosity. I raised my eyebrows, turned, and swiftly walked away. I had no interest in hearing about my brother's conquests, let alone watching them.

Not that I wasn't interested in women; I was. I blushed when the milkmaid would wink at me whenever she saw me and speak sounding as if she was always out of breath. The baker's daughter still rubbed up against me whenever she passed me in the tavern making me feel hot, but the passion was inevitably short-lived, and the conversation dwindled to uncomfortable silences that made me want to be alone. I guess I just thought when I was with a woman, I would feel... more. Sure, it made my body feel good for a while, but it wasn't enough. I imagined real love was excitement that didn't fade, a thrill in the company of another that only grew the more time and familiarity you shared.

I yearned to share my time with someone who wanted to talk about more than just village gossip. What about the stories the travelling merchants shared about the rest of Marieena? What about what lay in the depths of the forest we hadn't ventured to yet and the lands beyond the mountains? Were these not more interesting topics of conversation?

What intrigued me, and what no one seemed to talk about anymore, were the tales of Marieena's Enchantress. All who served her seemingly never returned home. It was said that their hearts had fallen so utterly in love with her beauty that they couldn't be parted from her, and so tales of her stayed with them. It was also said that it was her magic that made the island flourish; the trees, the flowers, the water — it all came from her. What tales did reach us, told of her dedication to the island. Year after year, she poured her magic into the earth to enrich everything we relied on to sustain ourselves.

The beauty of the island captivated me and made me feel overwhelming affection for the one who gave themselves to its care, and it was surrounded by this beauty I felt closest to her. Many of us, myself included, would give offerings to her in praise and thanks for all she gave us. We built a shrine in her honour in the centre of the village but I preferred to go to the riverbank to give her my offerings. Without her care, our land and animals would not thrive and our livelihood would be lost and for that, she would always have my devotion.

Each year, after we had taken the final cut of straw, I would weave an intricate wheat heart for her to express my thanks for a harvest successfully gathered. Taking this to the river and placing it gently into the water, I would watch it sail away, and imagine it making its long journey through the mountains to her where she would gaze upon it and feel my gratitude.

What little time I had to spare around my work on the land, I preferred to spend in the forest bordering one side of our farm. The forest was peaceful. Often the only sounds were my dull footfalls on the bed of blue-green pine needles, or gentle birdsong. If I was quiet enough, it was always a thrill to see the red deer herd making their way through the trees, heading towards the river, which ran wide, clear and smooth this far down the valley. I often sat on the rocky bank to put my feet in the cool water after a hot day in the fields. I had spent many a pleasant afternoon, feet in the water, face turned up, enjoying the heat of the sun on my skin.

It was the joy I felt every day in what she provided that made me so eager to know more about the Enchantress. To serve her was to offer yourself to her, utterly and without reservation, giving up all connections with your home until the day came that you returned. I hadn't met anyone who had been and come back, but the fanciful tales over the years ranged from her castle being guarded at night by a flock of silver gryphons that protected her while she slept to her skin being made of pearls. Having not heard these tales first-hand, it was hard to assess their validity..

Caring for the land and animals gave me a sense of belonging that I hadn't found in a person. I could walk across the land and feel utter peace, connected to everything and nothing all at once and feel comfort as if in company, but also happily alone at the same time. Time had no meaning out there, and what was in front of me was the only thing that mattered. Surely this is what I was meant to feel for the woman I was supposed to make my wife.

I tried to explain this to my father, but he just scoffed at such a notion.

"Just bed a pretty, sturdy girl that will please you when you need it and give you strong sons and handsome daughters."

I didn't bring it up with him again.

His relationship with my mother was not one I aspired to since I saw what it did to her. She spoke of his past romantic gestures with such a forlorn longing. It made me disappointed in him to see how she mourned the man she fell in love with, and made me all the more determined not to repeat his actions. In her quiet moments, my mother would gaze out of the cottage window with such a wistful look upon her gentle face. It tugged at my heart to see such longing. I had no intention of misleading a girl, no matter how pretty, into thinking I cared for her more than I did just so she would give me an heir to continue the farm and listen to me witter on in my later years.

From time to time, mother would tell me stories of the Enchantress and how she had cared for Marieena for as long as memory had been passed down. She was considered an ancient in this land, a being with no known beginning for she had always been, quietly caring for us through her devotion. Mother also impressed upon me the need to take care of the Enchantress. She told me there had once been a great band of Alphas, warriors, whose sole task it had been to protect our beloved Enchantress. Whether they had abandoned their duty or had been lost to their cause, no one knew, only that without them, she was alone and unprotected. Now it was up to those of us that she took care of to step up to the task as best we could. She said our offerings to the Enchantress and our adoration of her gave her heart and kept her strong.

But we had other pressing matters of late that demanded our attention as something was amiss. The talk among the villagers had become one of concern. Parts of the forest seemed to be dying. Not just the usual changes with the seasons, but fewer trees blooming each spring. The young trees looked to be withering, their leaves curling and the rich green tinged with yellow. The older trees bore less fruit than in previous years, affecting everyone's winter stores. Crops were taking longer to mature, and the fields furthest from the river seemed to yield less come harvest. I had thought they were just drying out but no matter how many channels and ditches I dug to direct the water towards that land, it made no difference.

The animals didn't seem to come out of the winters quite as well as in past years either; they were ribby, listless and their coats dull well into the spring months. These changes had most of the village grumbling, mainly about the price on market day, but they troubled the elders the most. They seemed to see more in these changes than just the increase in the price of a sack of spuds. Their concern was for the Enchantress, as was mine. I had watched this land adjust through many years of changing seasons, but something about this felt different, and my thoughts always seemed pulled back to her.

The mutterings from the council meetings postulated the idea of sending someone from Harth to the Enchantress's castle to offer themselves for service. It had been many years since someone had left on that journey, and some considered it a waste of council time to even discuss it, but when pressed on the extent of our crop issue they had no solution. Many others talked about going to her castle, but few were brave enough to actually leave. The arduous journey and the unknown once they reached her castle seemed too much, and the call of the comforts of home too great. These folks considered it just a bad year and seemed happy in their ignorance so I didnt press them. Admittedly, to give up everything you had worked for and leave it all behind was a tough ask, particularly for those such as myself, who took care of a family business that had taken generations to build, and occupied every waking moment to maintain. But, without the Enchantress, none of this would be possible, the land would be barren without her. Our good fortune was ours only by her grace.

My father disagreed. He would laugh at the stories mother would tell and get angry at me for laying our prosperity at the Enchantress' feet.

"It's my back and the backs of my father and grandfather that built this farm! What does she who sits in a mighty castle know about the physical labour it takes to work this land each day?! Magic? Huh, I have seen no evidence of such a thing."

"What of those times when the river flooded just as the crops were at risk of failing? What of the times when our animals seemed to pull through when we had done all we could and it seemed they would be lost to us?" I insisted.

He would have none of it. My mother would gently pat my arm and turn me away, knowing I would never convince him, knowing that she herself had tried and failed many times before.

Whether it was believed to be by the Enchatress' grace or the effort of my back, I was well-respected for the prosperity of our farm. I had worked it all my life alongside my brothers and under my father's not-so-patient guidance. Despite his eternal frown, I had worked hard at my chores, not only to make him proud but also out of the satisfaction it gave me. My brothers were less enthusiastic and gradually drifted away from the farm for other more appealing work, which made the decision of who would take over the farm when my father's health suddenly declined, despite my young years at the time, a relatively straightforward one.

It was this lifetime of dedication to the land that made it clear in the elders' minds who would be the best suited to make the journey to the Enchantress. It was to their great relief when the day I came of age in my twenty-first spring, that that was the decision I made. Leaving the land and animals I had tended to my whole life was no easy decision, but I owed this rich land to her, so it was my duty to repay her devotion with my own.

I bid my family farewell, setting off before sunrise on the long journey to the Enchantress's castle. The exact location of which was not known, only that it lay in the forest beyond the Green Mountains. Knowing the river headed that way, and having a compulsion to stay near the water,

I followed its course deeper into the forest and beyond the borders of Harth. This was land I had never crossed before, each step taking me further away from all that was familiar. The unease in the pit of my stomach intensified when I reached the mountains. The river bank disappeared where the water cut a gorge through the mountains leaving no way to continue along its course so I had been forced to take the mountain path. The steep incline and loose shale made progress slow. It took several days of continuous travel, and some uncomfortable nights sleeping on the mountainside, to finally make it to the top. I was bruised and aching but had no intention of stopping.

Pushing myself to my feet, the wind rose up to greet me, sucking the breath from me and nearly toppling me over. Catching myself, I forced myself up to standing so I could look down into the valley beyond. I stood seemingly on top of the island and relished its magnitude. Vast mountains covered in purple heather ran on either side of the valley, sharp and thick, hugging the deep, vast forest that nestled in the valley below. The wide, foaming river carved a path through the trees and disappeared into its depths.

Coming back to myself, I looked around for a path down. I was relieved to see this side of the mountain had thin goat trails that zigzagged their way down to the valley floor and picking the widest, I carefully began my descent. As the sun made its journey across the sky, I didn't seem to make it far, for much of the track I had to go down backwards so as not to overbalance myself.

The sun's journey across the sky was all too swift and my progress slow. All too soon, darkness crept over the mountain and I was forced to make camp. A small, rocky outcrop provided a welcome waystation for the night. My supplies of bread and cheese had run out days ago so supper was the same dried meat and wrinkled apples I had eaten since, but my empty stomach was thankful for them, though I hoped the forest would yield something fresh. My water supplies were much depleted too. For most of the journey I had followed the river so I had been able to refill my waterskins each day, but my trek over the mountains had been slow and I'd needed to ration what little I could carry to make it last. If it took me much longer to reach the river again I'd run out entirely.

With the last light, I tried to put these concerns aside for now and collected what dry moss and twigs I could find scattered about and managed to get a small fire going in a hollow in the back wall of the outcrop. It provided little heat, but anything against the dropping temperature was a relief. Untying the sheepskin from my pack, I lay it out on the ground near the fire. My body screamed, pain shooting through my back as I lay flat and stretched out after a day hunched. After a minute, the tension eased and I turned my back to the fire and curled up. Looking out into the clear sky I thought on my journey's end, slipping into sleep trying to imagine what the Enchantress truly looked like.

Chapter 3

Enchantress

I feel it in the water, a feverish swell of anticipation that rushes towards me.

My body and mind submerged in its embrace, devoid of thought and open only to my base intuition, welcomes the approach of an unknown familiar.

Something is coming.

Chapter 4

Rook

Mist hung over the mountains the next morning. Shivering, I curled tighter, giving my body a few more minutes rest before tentatively stretching out. My leg muscles were tight, and my hip and shoulder sore, having been slept on all night. Grumbling like an old man, I pushed myself up to standing, scruffing my hand through my hair and shuffled to the other side of the outcrop to relieve my bladder.

Breakfast consisted of the last two wrinkled apples in my pack. While I savoured my meagre breakfast, legs dangling over the edge of the outcrop, I scanned what I could see of the mountain below, the rest of the valley covered in mist, my mind wandered to my journey's end.

Will I reach the castle before day's end?

I knew the castle lay in the forest in the forest, but where exactly, no one had been able to tell me. I had been so eager to make it this far, guessing the mountain would be the toughest part of the journey, but now nerves knotted my stomach as I considered the unknown path beyond here.

"Well, too late now," I huffed to myself.

Bundling my pack in my sheepskin, I secured it to my back and continued my descent. The midday sun was burning the back of my neck when I finally skidded to the valley floor. The river suddenly looked wider and the trees taller. The river cut a wide fast-flowing course across my path to the forest, foaming and crashing over unseen rocks.

"Ah, shit."

The only bridge in view looked as though it was ready to release its hold on the bank and let itself be swept downriver. Moss decorated the wooden bracing posts and the rope lashing them to the rail was frayed and weather-worn. Footboards were missing, and others cracked. Taking hold of the bracing posts, I reached a foot to the first board and pushed on it. It groaned, louder still the more weight I put on it.

"Are you going to hold my weight?" I muttered, sceptical as to whether or not I'd make it to the opposite bank dry.

Weary from my journey so far, the prospect of searching the riverbank for another bridge that either did not exist or if it did was as weather-worn as this one, was not an appealing one. The sun danced on the surface of the water, creating an ever-changing pattern of light and darkness that would have seemed inviting had the blackness not hinted at just how deep the water was.

Decision made, I started across the bridge. The boards gave slightly under my weight, restricting my pace, but thankfully remained intact. The water rushed by below me, the waves spraying me with tiny droplets. I trained my eyes ahead. Feeling my way across the boards with my feet, fearing to look down would affect my balance. But the movement of the water kept catching my attention. Standing over it now, it appeared thicker and churned in a way that created colours I hadn't seen before, with a shimmer to them that didn't look quite right. The water rolled with the consistency of thin butter, shining in the sun and then plunging to darkness. It demanded my attention, lured me to pause and take it in, lean closer, touch it. How would it respond to my fingers?

A bird screeching overhead.

"Fuck!"

I jolted back from the water, wobbling as I regained my balance. I had been pitched so far forward over the side of the bridge I was only inches from the water.

Damn it! What the hell?!

Straightening, I refocused on the bridge with a determined effort to stay upright. Some gaps were several boards wide, and more than once my foot slid as I landed on the next damp board taking my breath away and forcing me to lean harder on the wobbly handrail. My legs were shaking when I finally hit solid ground on the other side.

The forest appeared brighter with closer proximity. From this side of the bridge, the bark of the trees seemed to move, its woven patterns winding in intricate knots and deep crevices. The gnarled fingers of their branches reached for me, as if in welcome. Figures appeared and disappeared in the motes of sunlight filtering through the canopy. Did the song come from them? They danced along the mossy forest floor, beckoning me.

Is this the effect of the Enchatress' magic?

The forest back home felt welcoming and familiar, but here the trees seemed to lean as I walked between them, as if to embrace me, their rustled greeting dulling the voice of the river. Through the overgrown foliage in jarring contrast to the tree greenery, bright blooms of pink and yellow clung to stone. Their matted wines created a lace curtain, veiling the wall. Their perfume ladened the breeze with an unfamiliar sweet perfume. Holding my hands up to shade my eyes, I followed their assent up the walls which, like the trees seemed intent on touching the sky.

I stopped abruptly, catching myself mid-stride when I noticed a set of double wooden doors set back into the wall.

I had made it.

The thought came easily, unconscious but without doubt. I had made it to the Enchantress' castle. The breeze seemed to push me forward as if in confirmation, encouraging me on when my nerves suddenly failed me. Concern hollowed my stomach. What if I had made a mistake? Who was I to just turn up like this? What if she turned me away? No, I couldn't leave. I couldn't return home with nothing to show for my long journey and still carrying my concerns. I resolved to plead with her to let me stay if necessary. I would sleep outside the door if I had to. I'd stay as long as it took for her to give me a chance to prove my usefulness to her, in whatever form that took. We needed her, as she needed us, me.

I stepped up to the doors and with a slightly shaking hand lifted the large knocker and banged it firmly. A minute went by, nothing. I knocked again, but nothing. The longer I stood the more my nerves set my miund to worrying who might eventually answer. Maybe the herd of silver gryphons, claws raised sharp beaks snapping, ready to rip me open, it suggested.

"Idiot," I muttered to myself.

I lifted my hand to knock again when a small window in one of the doors slid open. Penetrating green eyes stopped me short and held me fixed in place. All thought abandoned me as her gaze burned through me, no accusation in it, but full of fire nonetheless. The breeze picked up just enough to gently catch a lock of her hair and slide it over her cheek. I watched as it caressed her face and then fell back into place, framing her delicate features. Not an unkind face but certainly not one to cross. This is not how I imagined a silver gryphon to look.

"Good morning friend, can I help you?"

"Uh, yes," I stammered, taking a moment to regain my composure, "I'm here to offer myself into the service of the Enchantress."

I quickly brushed my hand through my hair to comb it straight with my fingers and tugged at the hem of my tunic, hoping I was at least half presentable and making a good first impression. Despite tier being no accusation in her stare, I brushed at the dirt I imagined coated every inch of my travel-weary body.

Her green eyes lit up and looked me up and down. "Please come in," she replied, smiling now.

The window slid shut, and a moment later, the door groaned as it slowly opened. I stepped over the threshold into a blessedly cool antechamber, dim by comparison to the brightness of the forest but still providing enough light to appreciate the figure before me. The gatekeeper stood a little shorter than me. Her silver hair fell in waves to her hips and her slender frame was wrapped in a delicate silk dress of pale green that cascaded to her ankles. She either didn't expect trouble from the visitors she welcomed, or she was capable of dealing with them despite her flimsy attire.

"What should I call you stranger?" she asked, tilting her head slightly, fixing me with her sharp eyes.

"Uh, Rook. My... My name is Rook."

"Rook, it's a pleasure to meet you. This way."

She led me into a square courtyard, which was divided into four quadrants with paths that made a cross through the middle. Large trees ablaze with orange leaves and heavy with pink peaches adorned each bed, boxed in by full blueberry bushes. In the centre of the courtyard was a large, deep pond, its smooth surface broken by the flashing white scales of fish caught in the sunlight and the trickling water from a fountain. The fountain was comprised of a pink, rough-cut stone, large enough to likely take the strength of many men to lift it. Water bubbled from the top of the stone and trickled down its grooves and slopes into the pond, making a pleasant sound.

"So tell me about yourself, Rook." The gatekeeper's gentle voice sent a delicate tremor through my chest. Regaining myself, I replied, "I'm from Harth. It's a village south of the Green Mountains."

"Beyond the Green Mountains? That's quite a journey."

"It was, but it was a journey I was eager to make."

"And why is that?" she asked, turning to look at me, a slight frown marring her face.

Her protective instinct for the Enchantress warmed me to her.

"It's our village," I replied, "The land is struggling."

Her frown deepened and I feared she would dismiss me so I quickly continued. "At first, we dug ditches thinking the fields were just drying out but then the forest began to suffer too. We have sent offerings and prayers to the Enchantress. When this had no effect, the elders were concerned for the Enchantress. They told us of a time when volunteers were sent to serve her, to assist with her duties to the island. It was my honour to offer myself for the task."

Her expression smoothed. "Is that so? And why do you consider it an honour?"

Thinking a moment, I replied, "The Enchantress has done so much for me and my family. Our farm has always been prosperous and I feel indebted to her for that. But more than that, it's this place, this island, our home. If she is in need of help to sustain it, I will do all I can."

She paused and turned to me, considering me for a moment. The green of her eyes seemed to swirl, putting me in mind of a summer leaf caught in a swift river. I found myself drawn in, tracking their movement, and unable to look away from the strangeness of them. When my face suddenly heated, I realised I had been staring at her and quickly looked away.

The gatekeeper lead me through a narrow, high-ceilinged antechamber and out into a meadow beyond. The meadow was enclosed by the castle walls and was full of wildflowers with mature trees dotted throughout. A short distance away, a red-haired man picked flowers, adding them to a bunch in his hand. Wearing only a pair of loose breeches, his bare torso was twisted away from us, exposing defined muscles along his arms and shoulders. His thick hair hung loose, falling down his back, the ends brushing the top of his pants. He turned to look at us as we approached.

"Mistress. For you." He inclined his head for a moment before handing the silver-haired beauty the bunch of flowers.

I froze.

Mistress?

This is...her. The Enchantress.

My mind went blank and words failed me.

"Thank you, Gerard. How sweet." The affection in her voice was thick. "This is Rook, he has come to serve here. Would you mind settling him in and bringing him to me in the hall a little later?"

"Of course, Mistress."

She turned to me. "It was a pleasure to meet you, Rook. Gerard will see to your needs for now and we will talk more later." She gifted me a radiant smile as she walked away.

Still frozen and unable to speak, I turned to Gerard. His smile was a sympathetic one. "Nice to meet you, Rook. Have you had a long journey?"

"That...that was...the Enchantress?"

"It was."

"I would have said...more, had I known it was her."

He put a hand on my shoulder, squeezing it lightly. "Don't worry, there will be time for that this evening. Come with me, you must be hungry and in need of some rest."

Gerard led me across the meadow to the bathhouse. A wide sunken pool took up the centre of the room. Flowers floated on the surface, releasing their sweet aroma into the air.

"Here we are. There is a bed chamber beyond that door where you will find fresh clothes. Feel free to take a bath and rest a while. If you are hungry the kitchen is at the end of the corridor. Evan will have laid out the afternoon spread so help yourself. I will come for you in a couple of hours and take you to our Mistress. For now, she requires my attention for today's offering so I will take my leave."

"I should have said more to her," I blurted out. "I should have told her...more. Please can you take me to her now, Gerard?"

He gave me a kind smile. "You will see her soon enough. Rest now and I will bring you to her later."

He patted my shoulder and left, striding across the meadow. I stood in the archway of the bathhouse watching him leave.

I should have said more to her. Told her of our devotion to her, told her that if there was anything we, I, could do, we would do it for her. After all she has done for us, she deserves no less.

I couldn't have her think I hadn't shown her the level of respect that she deserved. When Gerard was a good distance away, I stalked after him across the meadow. He would lead me to where the Enchantress was and I could make a fresh start with her. He headed towards a small copse of trees set in the centre of the meadow. Pausing at the tree line, I waited until he was out of sight before following him along the path. There was a small clearing at the centre of the copse and a group of people were sprawled on the grass. As I approached, I saw the people in more detail and flushed when I realised they were in varying stages of undress and were touching one another. Some men wore only their breeches, varying amounts of downy chest hair and muscular torsos on display, while most of the women were entirely naked, their bare shapely limbs dappled in the sunlight that filtered through the leaves.

A jolt of desire surged through me when my eyes caught on the figure of the Enchantress nestled in the centre of the group, reclined on a small mound of moss, glowing as if light radiated from her. The others blurred in the peripheral of my vision as my attention was held only by her. Her wavy hair shone like clear water, flowing over her body and rippling in the breeze, glinting silver. The sunlight gave her pale skin a shimmer as if brushed in gold where it found the elegant contours of her face.

I stood, frozen in the shade of the partly shadowed path, somewhat regretting my haste to go after Gerard but unable to tear my gaze away from the Enchantress as she lay sprawled in utter grace in what seemed like a throne of trees and beautiful bodies.

As Gerard approached her, she cast her eyes to him and smiled warmly when he took her hand and gently placed a kiss upon her palm before moving to stroke the hair of a blonde woman who was sitting astride a sandy-haired man. Looking back to the Enchantress, I started when her eyes hit mine. They blazed with such passion that my body heated and my breeches felt suddenly tight. She seemed to study me, her eyes roaming my body. My tongue darted over my lips as her eyes bore even more intently into mine, a smile spreading across her face as I managed to hold her gaze. Raising her hand, she beckoned me forward.

Running my sweaty hand through my hair, I stepped into the small glade and tried to think of what I should say to her. With each heavy step, my mind failed to gather my thoughts cohesively. My heart hammered as I moved closer to her and I felt a panic rising. Glancing briefly at the others in the group, I fumbled for my words as I dropped to my knees, head bowed and stammered through my greeting.

"Forgive my intrusion and haste to present myself to you, Enchantress, fair Mistress of Marieena. I have travelled far to get here in the hopes of serving you. I have heard tales of your beauty, but none come close to conveying your radiance."

I knelt, looking at the ground for what felt like an eternity. My knees ached, but I didn't dare shift to try to rearrange myself, concerned my shuffling would not win her favour. Slowly, concerned by the lengthy silence, I lifted my eyes to look into hers, wondering what her reaction would be to my words. She was running the nail of her thumb along her bottom lip and looking at me with a curious expression.

"Such pretty words and such passion for one so young."

Uncertain if by passion she meant my desire to serve her or my body's response to her, I remained silent, searching her face and praying that she would not send me away.

She cocked her head to the side, her green eyes glowing as I stared, waiting.

"You are bold to have come to me this way. It shows a strength of will that I admire. But we will discuss this more at the appropriate time. Return to the bathhouse. Gerard will bring you to me this evening."

Relieved not to be dismissed from the castle, I stumbled away, nearing running back to the bathhouse.

Chapter 5
Rook

Gerard led me through the castle, explaining the formalities of what was about to happen.

"Mistress will receive you in the main hall to discuss what would be expected of you if you are invited to stay."

"Yes, Sir."
"Gerard, please," he replied, the soft timbre of his voice lifting as he smiled.

"Gerard. Thank you," I replied, grateful for his reassurance.

"After your meeting, you're free to leave, though I do hope you will stay. You're a bold lad." His eyes caught mine, eyebrows raised.

Shame burned my face. "I'm sorry about... earlier. You told me to wait. I had no right to follow you, or be a part of..." Not knowing how to word what I had witnessed, I fell silent.

"There is no need for apologies. Your bold nature serves you well. Mistress is intrigued by you."

Double doors opened into a vast hall with a dais set at the far end. Columns that looked to be trees stood sentry on either side of the hall, six in total, reaching up to the ceiling and spreading their canopy wide across the room. On closer inspection, I was amazed to realise they were indeed living trees, rooted into the stone floor that had been built around them. Tall windows were set between each of these majestic pillars, coloured with the fading light of sunset.

We stopped a few feet short of the base of the dais where the Enchantress sat upon a throne of sorts, although it was unlike any I could have imagined. A cluster of silver birch trees, rooted into the floor, were woven through each other, creating a natural seat in which the Enchantress sat, before reaching high up above her, splaying in a crest. Her silk dress fell over her feet and rippled across the floor around her while her shoulders were covered by a cape of light grey fur. Embodying her status as Enchantress of Marieena, I wondered how many had stood in awe of her, eagerly awaiting her decision.

She smiled as we waited in silence before her. "Greetings, Rook. I want to offer you my apologies for my deception earlier when I met you at the gate. I find people act differently around me once they know who I am and I wished to gain an unbiased impression of you. I hope you can forgive me."

"Of course... Mistress."

Her eyes blazed a moment at my response before continuing. "Tell me why you wish to serve me."

Taking a deep breath, I paused a moment to gather my thoughts before replying, "Through your generosity, you have cared for me every day of my life, seeing to it that the land provides for me and my family. Should you now need more of me, I will happily return your devotion with my own."

She stilled, a shadow crossing her face for a moment leaving a fleeting expression I was unable to read before she recovered herself. "Devotion takes many forms, Rook," she replied. "Everyone who serves me has a role within the castle depending on what they are skilled at, be it baking, weaving or tending crops. The purpose of this service is to feed my magic through their love. Love through their devotion to their duties and to me." She paused, giving me a moment to reflect. "Others from across the land do this through their prayers and the offerings they send to me or leave for me in their shrines. Their love comes to me and strengthens my magic so I can share it with the land."

It is love that supports her magic.

"There is, however, a stronger form of love that those who serve here share with me." With no effort, her gentle voice held me rooted in place, her authority and my need for her every word absolute.

"This is the physical love they share with me, and each other."

Physical love?

As in... the copse?

"Should you decide that you do not wish to extend the level of your devotion to such then you are welcome to return home and resume your life. But those who reside here give themselves to me, all of themselves, and to serve here, you must do the same."

Devote myself to her.

My desire stirred, imagining that she could possibly mean that she would want me to bed her.

Surely not.

I had never doubted my intention to give myself over to her service but I hadn't imagined that service would include physical love. Surely there were many others more worthy to serve her in this regard than I. A man though I was, I was inexperienced in such matters.

But if she asked it of me...

There was no denying the beauty of her, and the response my body had to her presence. Just standing before her heated my body and turned my thoughts to how it might feel to run my hands over her pale, slender body. But beyond her body was a power, a strength unlike I had ever known. She had a certainty in her manner that gave me trust in her judgment.

"I am yours, Mistress."

"Then I welcome you, Rook. Attend your duties and we will talk again soon."

Years of considering this moment, countless imaginings as to how this meeting could play out, and finally I had gained the acceptance I was desperate for. I was hers.

"Come on, boy. I will show you to your room." Gerard inclined his head to the Enchantress and led me from the hall.

Chapter 6
Enchantress

This one intrigues me.

I have met many through my years, but this one is something entirely new.

There is a shimmer to his body that is different from the others. He has an innocence to him that shines through. His desire to please and show his love is evident in even his smallest gestures.

There is usually a look of awe on their faces when they meet me for the first time. It is endearing and fills me with gratitude for their love, but this...this one has fire in his eyes, and I can feel my body respond to it.

He harbours a fierce passion that even those who have spent many years with me do not possess.

Chapter 7
Rook

Shafts of light stretched across the ceiling. I lay still for a moment, enjoying the warmth and letting the sleepy fog in my mind dissipate. When the haze cleared I sat up and cast my eyes over my new bedchamber. It was a novelty to have a bedchamber to myself; having so many brothers had always meant sharing with at least one of them.

The embers of the fireplace still glowed and I was thankful for the kettle of warm water as I washed and shaved. It was a relief to get rid of the days-old stubble from my face. In the chest at the foot of my bed, I found several sets of linen breeches, light summer tunics, thick woollen socks, and a leather belt. Pleased to have something other than my own journey-tired clothes to wear, I admired the quality of the cloth as I slipped the fresh clothes on. Boots laced, I stepped out into an empty hallway and glazed around trying to remember my way to the kitchen when I nearly walked into Gerard coming round the corner.

"Good morning, Rook. I was just coming to find you. Hungry?"

"I am, but was just getting my bearings."

"Come on, my boy, this way. Evan will be expecting you in the kitchen shortly to discuss your duties but first, let's get you fed."

Gerard led me down the stairs and through a large, open hallway which had several doors leading off it. The ceiling towered two storeys above. I craned my neck to take in the depictions displayed across it. A large sun was painted in the centre with rays splaying out on all sides, reaching out to a border of trees.

The kitchen had a vast open stove below the chimney in the far corner to the left, blackened from years of use. Two long tables ran down the centre of the room, with benches on either side. All around the room were workbenches, heavy with produce. The huge spread consisted of cheese, preserves, fruit, yoghurt, milk and fresh bread; the smell of which made my mouth water and my stomach grumble.

Gerard chuckled. "Evan is up with the sun to make the bread each morning and lay out the breakfast spread, but there is always something in the larder, so help yourself anytime."

Sat at the table on the right was the blonde-haired lady I recognised from the copse and a black-haired man. They were deep in conversation when Gerard and I approached.

"Rook, meet Grace and Barden."

"Morning! Lovely to finally meet you, Rook!" said Grace in a bright, lyrical voice.

"Nice to meet you too," I replied, smiling at them both, taking a chunk of bread from the spread and pulling the butter towards me.

Gerard squeezed the shoulder of the black-haired man as he passed him. Barden stroked his arm in return as Gerard moved around the table to kiss Grace and seat himself next to her, leaning to pick an apple from the spread. They clearly all shared a closeness, a familiarity in their touch, that came from more than just friendship. Mistress spoke of their desire for each other but was it just physical, an effect of providing intimate offerings to her, or something more?

I sat beside the black-haired man, who wore a pair of navy breeches and nothing else.

"Well, good morning, handsome." Barden leaned back from the table, exposing his smooth chest and slim, athletic frame. "Very nice to meet you, Rook."

His smile broadened as he offered me his hand to shake.

Did he just forget his tunic this morning?

"You too." I took his surprisingly soft hand and squeezed it, noting his flattery and holding it in my mind as I returned a smile.

"My, my, such a strong grip." He reached forward to run his fingers along my arm as he spoke.

Goosebumps peppered my skin where his hand had been. Barden's touch wasn't unwelcome, I just hadn't experienced this kind of intimate touch from a man before. My father had always emphasised the purpose of relations was for the production of children. All else was just distraction from necessary work.

"Alright, Barden. Put the boy down," came Gerard's deep, reprimanding tone.

"Oh, must I? Just look at him though! He's so pretty."

"He sure is, but we don't want to frighten the lad, do we?"

"No, I guess not," said Barden in a mock wistful voice, stroking my arm one last time before winking at me and returning to his breakfast.

My face prickled but I was surprised to find I was quite delighted by Barden's affections. Although I hadn't found myself feeling attracted to another man before, when I studied Barden, I found myself appreciating just how handsome he was. His black hair was short around his ears, but the rest was long and stuck in different directions. He had a strong jaw with smooth, cleanly shaven skin and a long, straight nose. His deep blue eyes looked like marble up close, with swirls of different shades of blue running through them.

It wasn't just his face that I found appealing. He had a way about him, a confidence in how he held himself, a sureness in his manner. I could see why the Enchantress would want him here, with her.

Does he serve the Enchantress through the intimacy he shares with the others or... directly?

"Are you staring at me, pretty boy?" Barden said, pulling me from my thoughts. "Because if you are, then I'd be inclined to return the favour." Barden's eyes slid over my thighs, his lower lip held in his teeth.

"Oh, sorry," I mumbled, turning back to the table and my bread as if it suddenly required my undivided attention to be eaten.

"Oh, no need to apologise, gorgeous. You look all you want," he purred with a mischievous grin.

Grace threw an apple at Barden, hitting him in the chest with it. "Leave him alone to eat his breakfast. Sorry, Rook. Barden is more lusty than the rest of us put together," she said in a loud mocking voice sticking her tongue out at him. Barden only winked at her in return.

A broad, blonde-haired man strode into the room. His chiselled face was all sharp angles and straight lines, his vast body nothing but muscle, all of which he held stiff and tall with an air of authority.

"Morning all." His voice was smooth but brisk as his black eyes scanned everyone. He seated himself next to Barden, the thin fabric of his breeches straining around his thick thighs, pulled tight by a cord around his tree trunk of a waist.

"Morning Evan," said Grace and Gerard simultaneously.

"Mmm, good morning, Evan," gushed Barden, his voice turning sweet as he leaned into Evan and put his head on his shoulder.

Evan reached his arm over to run his hand along Barden's jaw tilting his face up so he could gently kiss Barden on the lips. I couldn't help but stare, having never seen two men kiss in such a manner, their handsome faces locked together, eyes closed in a shared tender moment. Coming to myself I hastened to look away, not wanting to intrude.

There had been a couple of men back home who didn't court the young women, preferring to spend time with each other. The poor devils seemed to draw whispers wherever they went for it, despite never sharing more than a heated glance in public. It didn't bother me who they chose to spend their time with. They were friendly guys who worked hard, which should have been good enough for anyone.

"Hey precious," Evan whispered against Barden's lips, before sitting straight again and glancing over to me while pouring himself a cup of water from the jug on the table. "You must be Rook."

I nodded, smiling sheepishly, feeling intimidated as Evan shook my hand in his powerful grip. "Welcome. It's good to meet you... officially."

"Uh... nice to meet you too," I replied, feeling my face flush as my mind replayed details of the scene from the copse the day before. My eyes flicked to Barden for a moment who grinned and chewed on that damn lip of his again, no doubt knowing full well the cause of my discomfort.

"You are a much-needed pair of extra hands, I'll tell you. I manage the household and will assign you your duties, which you can start tomorrow once you have had some time to settle in." He helped himself to some bread and jam from the middle of the table.

"Yes, Sir."

"Oh my," Barden scoffed, looking up at Evan.

"Insatiable little beast," Evan muttered, squeezing Barden's thigh. "Don't start that now, the lad doesn't know what you're getting worked up about." Grace tittered and looked again at Barden. Fully aware I was missing something, I quietly ate my breakfast, intrigued to find out what exactly it was that eluded me.

"Well, the days getting on," said Gerard, "Grace, we best go if we are going to make it to the glade and back before midday."

He stood up, offered his hand to Grace, bid us all farewell, and left.

"Right, you." Evan roughly clamped his hand to the back of Barden's neck and pulled his face close. "Go to my room and wait for me." He looked deep into Barden's eyes and a wide smile spread across Barden's face.

"Yes, Sir," replied Barden, leaping up from the table and eyeing me once more before bounding out of the room.

"Never runs out of energy that one," chuckled Evan in his gruff voice, glancing at me.

Grinning back, I considered what it was men of a particular inclination might do to one another when they were alone. My mind wandered to my time in the barn with the baker's daughter. Would Evan and Barden do such things...to each other? My mind flashed with the image of Evan seated on a hay bale with Barden knelt between his massive thighs.

"So, your duties. Mistress tells me you were a farmer back home. Did you enjoy the work?"

"I... I did," I replied, stuttering in my attempt to pull my mind from the barn. "The role of managing the family farm was passed down to me when my father retired, and I was happy to accept it.

"Excellent, just what we need. In that case, you will help tend the crops in the paddocks. Grace does this alone at the moment, and she would welcome the help. The east paddock has been fallow for a few years now and needs clearing before the horses can plough it so that will be your task for now. Grace is helping Gerard today, but when she goes out to the paddocks tomorrow she will show you where everything is."

I nodded, pleased to be given a job I knew I would enjoy and, more importantly, do well to hopefully impress the Enchantress.

"Good lad. So, the day is yours to do with as you please. That door there will take you out into the meadow, and that door will take you to the library. If you need anything, just come back here. There is always someone popping in and out of the kitchen. Now, if you will excuse me, I have a lustful youth to attend to."

Evan stood, squeezing my shoulder before leaving the room.

# Chapter 8
Rook

Eager to see more of the castle, I followed Evan's directions to the library. The door from the kitchen opened onto a long corridor lined with windows that looked out onto the meadow. The sun was just visible over the castle walls flooding the meadow in warm light.

At the end of the corridor, a large wooden door stood slightly ajar, a smouldering log glowing in the fireplace on the far wall. The door groaned as I pushed it wide to step through into the vast room. On either side of the room, three levels of mezzanine floors stretched to the arched ceiling, with rows and rows of bookcases beyond their balconies. The shelves reached back to the castle's outer walls, to tall arched windows that flooded the vast room with light. I had never seen so many books. Our small bookcase in our cottage back home paled in comparison to this impressive collection.

On the ground floor a large square table where several books lay open. A narrow set of steps took me to the second level. Deep cushioned sofas were positioned under each window between the shelves, some still with a couple of books lying on them, one with someone snoozing with their face hidden under an open book, his long sandy hair spilling over the arm of the sofa. Not wanting to disturb the sleeping figure, I crept to the nearest shelf, selected a book, and crept out again.

Sunshine flooded the meadow. Blinded as I stepped out, I closed my eyes for a moment and let it warm my face, breathing in the smell of the flowers that floated thick in the air. The top fields of our farm would be busy with the first of the spring lambs making their appearance. This would usually be one of the busiest times of year back home so it was odd to consider having time to myself. Laying down in the long grass, hands behind my head, I closed my eyes. Even with no one else around the meadow wasn't silent, birds gently sang overhead, and an insect buzzed somewhere nearby. After the barren winter months, these insistent signs of life were always welcome.

Life seemed to bloom brighter here, and not just in the trees and the grasses but in the people themselves. The changing seasons showed the bond all aspects of the natural world shared, and the people here seemed to share it too. Their manner with each other was so at ease, I could almost feel envious of them. There was a confidence that radiated through them all that paralleled that of their Mistress. It was a symbiosis I longed for beyond the land I had so lovingly tended. I was keen to see the paddock I would be taking care of alongside Grace. Eager as I was to get started on my duties, I could wait another day. Opening the little book I had picked up from the library, I found it was a book of poetry.

> *There is a pleasure in the pathless woods,*
>
> *There is a rapture on the lonely shore,*
>
> *There is society, where none intrudes,*
>
> *By the deep sea, and music in its roar:*

I love not man the less, but Nature more.

LB

The warm sun, the soft grass on my back and the buzzing insects were all lulling me with their contentment. My eyes drooped as I tried to read the rest of the page. I hadn't realised I had fallen asleep until a chuckle woke me. Lifting my hand against the high midday sun, Barden's figure came into view. He was sitting right next to me.

He grinned. "You snore like a dog."

"How exactly do I snore like a dog?" I laughed, craning to look at him.

"You do little twitches and grumbles as if you are chasing something. It's adorable."

"How long have you been there?" I asked, sitting up and rubbing my eyes as much to disguise my enjoyment of his flattery as to rub the sleep from them.

"Long enough to know you read poetry." He gestured to the open book lying next to me in the grass. "Tristan enjoys poetry too but I prefer straight forward stories myself. If you have something to say just get on and say it."

"Don't mince your words, you mean? Just come out and call the new guy handsome, huh?" I replied, raising my eyebrows at him. After a moment's pause, Barden burst into a hearty laugh.

"Exactly!"

I couldn't help but laugh too. His face was beautiful when he smiled, he did so so unashamedly. Despite his flirtations, there was an innocence to him, a child-like enjoyment of that around him that he expressed wholeheartedly.

"So, how long have you been in service here?" I asked.

"I have spent five glorious winters here," he replied. I was surprised by his answer and casting my eyes over him, wondered how he could have been here so long for one so young.

"Are you staring at me again, pretty boy?" Barden drawled.

"Sorry, it's just... How old are you?"

"I have seen twenty-three winters. Evan brought me here after meeting me in my home town of Tride."

"Whereabouts is that?"

"It's only half a day's journey northwest of here."

Eager for any stories from other villages, I asked, "What was it like growing up there?"

Smiling, Barden continued, "I had a privileged life being the youngest son of the Weaver family. We bought raw silk and unprocessed flax and turned them into bolts and sometimes garments, though we mostly sold the bolts at market. My sister is a seamstress, she taught me to sew. Each festival she made a dress as an offering to the Enchantress and we would journey here to present it to her."

"So you visited the castle before you came to live here?"

"Yep. It was always an exciting trip to make. My father saw how much I enjoyed it and allowed me to come, along with my sister who had made the dress of course. She had no interest in entering service here since she was so happy back home but I needed a new start."

"Why is that?" I asked.

Barden hesitated for a moment, then glancing over my shoulder, held his hand up in greeting to someone. Turning I saw a woman with a mass of red curly hair striding towards us. "Brianna, come and meet Rook."

Brianna shook my hand as firmly as any man ever had.

"Good day to you, Rook. It's good to meet you." She wore loose breeches and a loose tunic with a belt of woven leather wrapped around her waist. Over her shoulders, she wore a short, fur cape. Crouching next to Barden she removed her cape and showed it to him. "I was just coming to find you, sweet boy. This rip up the back of my cape keeps letting the rain in. I need it repaired before I next head out."

"I'll get right on it."

"Ah, you're a good lad," she said, scruffing Barden's hair. "Right, best get the rest of my kit sorted then. Good day to you both." She stood and brushed the hair from her face, splitting it into sections and beginning to braid it as she strode away.

"She doesn't hang about does she?" I laughed.

"That she doesn't!" Barden chuckled. "She's our resident hunter so spends much of her time stalking through the forest which suits her nature."

Looking up, I spotted Gerard and Grace crossing the meadow, their arms full of something. "I best go and help them," I said, standing and dusting off my breeches, "Nice talking to you Barden."

"You too," he smiled, holding my gaze as he handed me my book. Butterflies danced in my stomach as I turned away.

The kitchen was welcomingly cool. Grace sat at the table with two large baskets of flowers beside her, busily plucking the petals from them, while Gerard gently scooped them into a wooden box lined with silk.

"They smell lovely," I said, sitting down at the head of the table between them. Grace beamed and leaning forward, gently kissed my cheek. "Don't they? I'll show you where they grow." She held a handful up for me to smell and smiled as I did. "Can I help?" I asked. Gerard squeezed my shoulder and gestured to the other basket, "If you'd like to start on them, that would be helpful."

"Will do. What are they for?"

"We dry the petals by adding rock salt to each box and then put them in the pool water. The salt is good for scrubbing and the petals give the water its fragrance," said Gerard.

"Huh, where do you get the salt from?" I asked.

"We trade items with the Northern villages."

"Oh," I said. "I spoke to the travelling traders who passed through Harth about the lands to the North but have never actually met anyone from the Northern villages."

"I think you will find you have," smiled Gerard. "I'm from a village in the north."

"Really? Where?"

"Scaw. It's a large mining village six days North of here. I ran a stud farm back home. I bred and trained the cart horses used for haulage. Then Mistress made me Horse Master when I pledged to serve here."

"We had an old gelding on my family's farm. He's a friendly old boy. I trained him myself, but he doesn't do much these days," I laughed.

"I can take you out to meet the horses in the morning if you like?"

Having missed my old companion pony back home, I was all too eager to meet the new horses I would work alongside. "I'd like that," I replied.

Gerard chuckled at my enthusiasm. "That's settled then."

"Can you tell me more about Scaw?" The travelling merchants would bring news with them but to them, one town was all but the same as the next town when you were spending most of your time in the market.

Gerard's smile broadened. "Of course. It's quite different from these parts. There are deep caverns in the mountains where we mine gems and minerals, including salt. The pink amethyst in the courtyard pond came from Scaw." He seemed to sit a little taller as he continued. "It took a sturdy cart and four of my strongest horses to get it here, but it was my honour to deliver it as a gift to our Mistress."

"You visited here before you were in the Mistress' service?" I asked.

"That is how I came to be in her service. I arrived after a long, slow journey. My horses were tired and in need of rest, and our Mistress offered for me to stay the night here. I fell in love with it all very quickly, and only hours after arriving, I was on my knees before the Mistress asking to stay here indefinitely. You must understand I had no family back home," he explained. "No one was waiting on me. I hadn't expected to fall in love with our Mistress, but I watched her, listened to her and marvelled at her insight." He looked away from me, a small grin spreading across his lips. The focus left his eyes as he continued to scoop unseen petals into the box, mind clearly elsewhere. He looked like a man in love.

I plucked the petals from the flowers and considered my own home. There was no one back home waiting for me either, not really. Mother lived in her books more than not these days so was little company to me anymore. I knew she loved me but that made it no easier to bear her sadness. My father and brothers loved me in their way, but we were very different people, a fact they seemed to enjoy tormenting me about. "Real men assert themselves. They push hard for what they want until they triumph and are respected for it." My father's words as he proudly watched my brothers compete in the summer games had long made me question our differences in what we most valued. I had no interest in competing with anyone for their respect. The farm was well-tended, and our family cared for. If my preference of spending my summer evenings reading or wandering the woods rather than wrestling in the games lost me the respect of my peers, then it wasn't a respect I felt I was missing out on. It did of course mean that finding enjoyable company was difficult.

"You will come to see, Rook, that this place is unlike any other," Gerard said. "And our Mistress is like no one you have ever met before. You will understand more and maybe feel the same as you spend more time here but should you have questions, you are always welcome to ask." His voice was quiet but gently probing, almost urging me to ask a question.

"Does...Uh...Does everyone have a partner here? Besides the Enchantress I mean." I gazed at the flower in my hand, before looking up at Gerard to gauge his reaction to what I hoped wasn't an impertinent question.

"They do. Some have several." Gerard nodded encouragingly. "We have all been lucky enough to meet someone here that we want to share more of ourselves with. Besides my love for our Mistress, I also have Grace and Tristan who are very dear to me." He reached across the table to rub Grace's hand.

"I see. And you have all been chosen by our Mistress to be here, to be close to her?"

"We have. She took time to know each of us before offering us a place here though. Our Mistress is particular about who she welcomes into the castle, Rook. It should bolster you to have been accepted so quickly into service."

I looked to Grace, who beamed at me and reached for my hand, squeezing it. "We are all different, but she sees something in each of us and that is a comfort," she whispered.

"What is it she's looking for?"

Grace raised her eyebrows and shrugged. "What are any of us looking for?" she asked before returning to her flowers.

I looked to Gerard, who smirked before going back to his task.

What are any of us looking for?

What am I looking for?

Did the Enchantress know the answer? Did she somehow know we were lonely and unfulfilled and wanted to care for us? Gerard spoke of his love for our Mistress, but what about the others? What about me? I hadn't been in love before, but this feeling I had for our Mistress was far beyond what I had ever felt for another. Was this love?

But, wasn't true love a mutual connection? Did she love us? Me? Maybe she just wanted to share her home with people who appreciated and loved the land as she did.

Or, maybe, she was lonely too?

Chapter 9

Rook

W ith further chores to attend to, Grace and Gerard left for the afternoon. With more time to myself, I returned to the library, hoping the sleeping figure had moved so I could take a better look around. As I slid the little book of poetry back into place, shafts of bright sunlight lit motes of dust through the three-story room. My love of poetry was my mother's doing. She had several of her own books of sweet rhymes that she would quietly read to me as a boy to lull me to sleep. Father didn't read, and if he had it certainly wouldn't have been poetry. But my mother adored it and shared that love with me.

Selecting a thick volume from the same shelf, I settled on one of the sofas and snuggled down to read.

Over and Over

My darling, without you, I merely exist from day to day,

No emotion, no depth, no ease of pain endured.

Our love was cast before this day,

In another time, we held each other,

We were one.

And now we have found once more,

The oneness we knew deep down to seek,

The love we hold for one another.

This is our predestined love that we feel,

The love that has already been felt between us.

Our journey of completeness has been reached before,

And will be reached over and over.

Do not fear death, my love, for I don't,

I know I will find you again.

SF

"I like that one too," said a quiet voice.

"Ah!" Nearly falling off the sofa in surprise, I turned to a mop of sandy hair. The man, who looked a similar age to me, had wide, innocent blue eyes that darted between me and the book.

"Sorry, friend." He chuckled, thrusting his hand to me. "Tristan, nice to meet you."

"Hi. Rook. Nice to meet you too." I replied, shaking his hand as I settled back into the sofa.

He leant over the arm of the sofa, his long, slender fingers pale as he rested his weight on them to crane over my shoulder. His intent gaze was not unlike a snowy barn owl with it's eye on a mouse. "What do you think of that one?" He gestured to the book in my hand.

"I like it, but then I have a weakness for romantic poetry." I smiled, running my hand through my hair, a nervous habit I couldn't seem to shake.

"Me too!" Tristan replied, the pitch of his voice increasing. "The others aren't so fussed about the romantic stuff. Gerard prefers the ballads of fantastical adventures, Barden prefers stories rather than poetry, and Evan just comes in here for new recipes."

"You seem to know much about everyone's preferences in reading material. Do you quiz them?"

He laughed. "I'm book keeper here."

"Ah, that makes sense."

"I was a bookmaker back home." He went on, lifting his legs over the arm of the sofa to perch on the arm. "My mother owned a bookshop. We traded in printed books but I also repaired damaged books too. A helpful skill with all the old books here."

"My mother was an avid reader and it's a pastime she passed on to me," I replied. "So, you have been here a while then?"

"Two years," he smiled, glancing around the bright room. "And I have barely made a dent in the repairs, I'll be here a while." The bright grin on his face told me just how he felt about that. "How about you? How are you settling in?"

"Honestly, I am surprised at how at home I feel here after such a short time. It is beautiful here, and everyone I have met so far has been friendly, and the Enchantress..." I trailed off.

Tristan gazed at me knowingly. "From what I hear, she rather likes you. Gerard says she has been a little out of sorts of late but has perked up since you arrived."

Heat spread over my face, and I glanced down at my book, a sheepish grin dancing across my lips. "I don't know what I have done to deserve her attention."

"Does there need to be a reason beyond that she likes you?" Tristan's sweet face searched mine, reassuring me and my wavering confidence.

"I suppose not."

Tristan and I spent the rest of the afternoon walking along the bookshelves together while he selected some of his favourite books to spread on the large table on the library's ground floor. Poetry, novels, history and mythology all piled up in thick, impressive volumes, bound in beautiful leather bindings.

Tristan leant his elbows on the table, surveying the stack of books we had gathered, his slender fingers stroking them. "Don't worry about putting them back when you are done. I ask everyone to leave their borrowed books here. That way, I can put them back and know they are all in their proper place." His voice took on a mock-reprimanding tone as he added, "I take my job as caretaker of the books here very seriously."

"Yes, Sir," I said, holding up both my hands playfully. "Although I took a book out to the meadow earlier, I hope that's not a problem."

"No problem at all," he replied. "You are welcome to take books out of the library as long as you take good care of them and don't go leaving them outside! Barden did that once and I have never forgiven him."

"Consider me warned!" I chuckled, half believing that he did in fact still hold the damaged book against Barden.

"Good. Now, since you enjoy romantic poetry so much, and I am eager to have someone to discuss it with, why don't you take this book with you and let me know what you think." He plucked a small navy book from the pile in front of him and handed it to me.

"I'll be done with this by bedtime," I replied, making a show of squinting at its few pages.

He raised his eyebrows at me. "If that's the case, you know where to find me."

"Don't you sleep?" I scoffed.

"I have found there are far more enjoyable pursuits to indulge in in the twilight hours."

He scooped up several books from the pile and headed towards the stairs. "You know where I am if you want me." Grinning, he turned and disappeared between the shelves.

Chapter 10
Rook

I couldn't sleep.

Despite the window having been dark for hours, I just couldn't seem to stop going over the events of the last few days. Finally being here, finally meeting the Enchantress and realising what was likely to be asked of me lingered constantly in the back of my mind. And then there was the castle itself, glorious and rich in all its aspects, including its inhabitants. These were people unlike anyone I had known before and I was eager to spend more time with them.

Not a surprise I couldn't sleep.

The book Tristan had suggested lay finished on the bed beside me. It told the poetic tale of a man who fell in love with a voice. The voice would sing to him when the moon was high but faded to nothing when the dawn appeared. Until one night when the moon fell from the sky and transformed into a beautiful woman who sang with the same voice. Tragically the lovers were never meant to be for the moon was needed in the sky. They enjoyed one night of passion together before she was drawn back to her lofty position, leaving her lover with a broken heart. He vowed never to sleep in the dark hours again so he could look upon her always.

I wonder if Tristan is still awake.

Grabbing the book to return to him, I eagerly crept downstairs to the kitchen, passing through the corridor beyond. The door to the library stood open, the lights dimmed but still bright enough for me to make out the book titles as I drifted along the rows. These books were beautiful, covers in deep reds and blues with gold writing and etchings along their spines.

Glancing around and not seeing Tristan, I headed towards the stairs. I marvelled at just how many books the Enchantress kept, slowly running my finger over their spines as I moved from one shelf to the next. Back in Harth, we had a small bookshop, set in a side room of the school. It only had new books when the merchants passed through, which was all too infrequently for me. I put a small amount of my wages aside each month for when they did so I could add to my collection, which was all too meagre, in my opinion. I had some firm favourites that I repeatedly read on dark winter evenings, but I was always keen to add new adventures and love stories to my shelf.

A murmuring of several voices from behind the next bookcase stopped me where I stood. I hadn't expected to meet anyone but Tristan. I suddenly had the feeling that I shouldn't be here. Ducking into the shadows and breathing as lightly as I could, I slowly tilted my head around the edge of the shelf to see who was there.

Gerard was sitting on a sofa facing the bookshelf I was hiding behind, his muscular thighs spread and his eyes cast down to something on the floor which I couldn't see. A hand suddenly appeared, tossing aside a bundle of fabric which landed near my feet, startling me. When I looked again, Tristan came into view, kneeling between Gerard's bare legs, running his hands up his thighs. He grinned up at Gerard and kissed the inside of his knee, working his way up.

What the...

Grace appeared, moving around the sofa behind Gerard, running her hands over his shoulders and down his chest. Gerard moaned and leaned his head back to kiss her.

Fuck, I shouldn't be here.

Tristan made his way further up Gerard's thigh. My jaw went slack at the sight of Gerard's long, hardening shaft as it came into view over his thick thigh.

I really shouldn't be here.

Tristan leaned in and touched his tongue to the very tip. Gerard's answering sharp inhale made my pulse quicken and my own cock twitch.

How open they are with their intimacy, just as in the copse.

Tristan grinned as he continued to lap at Gerard, squeezing his thighs as he did. Grace moved to kiss Gerard's neck while his hand played in her hair, rubbing his cheek against hers. So gently he nuzzled her face with his, burying his nose in her hair.

Tristan suddenly plunged forward, mouth wide, taking most of Gerard's shaft in his mouth. Gerard's head popped up, a growl emitting through his clenched teeth. A flush of heat radiated through my abdomen, and my growing desire made my breeches uncomfortable.

They don't know I'm here.

I shouldn't keep watching.

But I just can't tear myself away.

Tristan slowly slid his mouth off Gerard's now fully erect cock, both men grinning at each other as ropes of saliva bridged the gap. Tristan licked his lips to remove them, never taking his eyes from Gerard. At this, Gerard leant forward, grabbed Tristan's hair and pulled him forcefully up to kiss him. He thrust his tongue through Tristan's lips, devouring him, sucking his tongue into his own mouth. He grazed his teeth along Tristan's lips before pushing him back down between his legs. To see Gerard's usually calm and gentle demeanour taken over by this inflamed and forceful side, ravaged by lust, was exhilarating.

"Ah, Tristan," Gerard groaned, his chest heaving as Tristan kept his mouth locked around him.

A streak of possessiveness shot through me as I watched Gerard sink himself into my friend's mouth; that sweet mouth that had spoken poetry and stories to me all afternoon. I came here thinking he would be alone reading, glad of my company. Instead, Gerard is making him smile, like that, at him.

Alright, calm down.

What right have you to feel jealous of their intimacy?

"Is it my turn yet?" Grace whined, staring down at Tristan over Gerard's shoulder.

Tristan chuckled. "Come on then, sweetheart, he's slick enough for you now," he replied, holding a hand out to her.

Grace smiled and moved around the sofa and, with Tristan's help, straddled Gerard's lap. Pushing Grace's hips forward, so her breasts thrust into Gerard's face, Tristan buried his face between her legs. The sound of Tristan's tongue and Grace's moans pushed my desire closer to the edge. I stifled a grunt as I watched Tristan's jaw work hard against Grace's smooth skin and her sweet face gently contorted in pleasure. With his face still buried in her, Tristan pulled her hips down and lowered her onto Gerard's eager cock, pulling a deep groan from both of them as Gerard's full length disappeared.

A whisper of a noise behind me momentarily distracted me, but as Grace's hips began to ride Gerard and Tristan increased the pace of his tongue, it wasn't enough to pull my eager eyes away.

"Suck harder," Grace moaned to Gerard, his mouth clamped around her nipple. She pushed her breasts harder against his face as a flush of pink rose up her chest and neck. Gerard wrapped his arms around her, his hands eagerly roaming her back and gripping her hips, squeezing her flesh and pulling her to him as he ground into her.

Reaching behind her, Grace took hold of Tristan's hair and pulled him closer to her, making him gasp. Uncomfortable and hot, I couldn't help but attempt to rearrange myself, trapped as I was in my breeches.

From behind me, a hand suddenly slid over mine, and I froze.

Shit.

I'd been caught.

Lips made contact with the nape of my neck, raising goosebumps over my skin.

"Take it out." The silky voice of my Mistress commanded me, full of fire. "Keep watching and take it out," she purred, running her hand over my abdomen. "Serve your Mistress, as they do."

Hidden in the shadows with her at my back, watching the scene before me, my shame of being seen melted, replaced only by the need to do as she wished. Eager to obey and wound tight with desire, I quickly unlaced my breeches, my erection freeing itself easily.

"Stroke it," she breathed against my neck, sending more pulses of sensation through my chest. My jaw clenched as I rubbed myself in time with Grace's hips, now bobbing at a relentless pace on Gerard's lap.

Tristan's hands were wrapped tight around himself, veins raised along his arms as he vigorously rubbed himself.

"Don't they look beautiful?" whispered the Enchantress in my ear, her body appearing at my side, almost luminous in the fading light.

"You're beautiful," I replied, my body straining into her touch.

She smiled and kissed my neck again. "Stroke yourself to satisfaction, my darling. I want to see it."

Moaning at her words, unable to contain myself, I increased the pace of my hand to match my desire. She rubbed her hand over my chest and nuzzled her face into my neck, pushing my jaw away from her, so my eyes returned to Gerard, Grace, and Tristan.

The sound of skin on skin, with the accompanying groans of the others, spurred on my own pleasure and knowing the Enchantress, my Mistress, was watching sent me careering into climax. My hips ground the air as I heard the others reach their satisfaction. Looking down, I saw the Enchantress' cupped hand held just beyond the tip of my cock, her other hand gently stroking my neck.

"That's it, my darling. Give your seed to me," she purred.

Her words pushed me over the edge. I let out a strangled cry and watched as my ejaculation filled her hand, spurt after spurt of milky fluid covering her palm. She kissed my cheeks as I panted from the effort, my orgasm ripping through me, my face glowing under her attention.

"I hope... I pleased you, Mistress," I panted, squinting into her eyes as the last of my release emptied from me.

She lifted her hand, rolling my seed around her fingers and without breaking my gaze, brought her fingers to her mouth and slowly slipped each one inside, one at a time, one after the other. My knees nearly buckled. I had to lean against the bookshelf to keep myself upright as I watched her lovingly clean my seed from her fingers.

"Mmm, you did, my precious," she crooned, leaning in to kiss my cheek. "You did."

With a sly grin, she backed away, disappearing into the darkness, her eyes the last thing to disappear.

The heavy weight of my body suddenly returned to me, and, cock still in hand, I stumbled back and slid down the bookcase behind me. I sat for a moment, letting my breath ease.

Well, I'll sleep well after that.

Chapter 11
Rook

The following morning Grace led me to the East paddock which lay within the castle walls just beyond the courtyard, at the far end of the meadow. Struggling to not let images from the previous evening take over my mind each time I looked at her, I tried to focus my attention elsewhere. This land had been left fallow for a while as Evan had said. Varying flora stood waist deep and across the paddock several small trees and bushes had sprouted.

"I'm afraid it hasn't had any attention for quite some time. I've never worked this land. Evan has had me focus on the other paddock rather than spreading my efforts too thin and having little to show for it." Grace shrugged.

"It's not too big a problem," I replied, "It's had plenty of rest and been given time to store moisture ready for thirsty crops. These shallow-rooted wild plants take little from the land compared to crops so under all this the soil will be healthy."

"Well, you clearly know what you are talking about," she laughed. "It will be helpful to have you around when I need advice!"

"Anytime. Right, I'm going to need some tools."

"Of course, this way." She lead me back through the stone archway over the entrance to the East paddock. "There's a tool shed in the courtyard. Help yourself to whatever you need and if there is something you can't find just let me know."

"Thanks." The tool store was set into the castle wall beside the entrance to the East paddock. A faint smell of damp soil lingered and its low ceiling and small window made it dark and cool. It was well stocked and organised with rows of tools hanging from every wall and a sharp plough mounted on a wooden frame taking up the central floor space.

"I'll be across in the West paddock if you need me, I have some preparations to make before the ceremony at the shrine."

"Ceremony?" I asked.

"Yes, Mistress holds a ceremony each new moon to imbue the water with her magic. Hopefully, in a month you will be joining us," she said with a warm smile, as she turned and strode away.

A pang of disappointment hollowed my stomach at the thought of not being able to witness the ceremony. I was curious to know how exactly the Enchantress shared her magic with the rest of the island. But I knew I had to prove myself first and earn the right to be present at something so important.

Pulling out a scythe, some leather gloves and a bundle of rope, I headed back to the East paddock. Starting the day early while the sun still hid behind the trees meant the paddock was in cool, pleasant shade. I set to with the scythe, cutting a path along the castle wall, baling the flora into bundles as I went. By the time the sun was high enough to reach where I was working, I had made it to the end of the paddock with fresh stalks and a neat row of bundles standing along my newly cut path. Setting down the scythe, I rubbed the sleeve of my tunic across my sweaty brow and paused a moment to catch my breath.

"Well, that's impressive."

I looked up to see Barden striding along my cleared path, holding out a waterskin to me. "I didn't think you would make it to the end of the paddock before I finished repairing Gerard's breeches." He gestured up to a second-story window that stood open. "I might have been looking in on you while I was in the workshop."

"If I knew I had an audience I would have put on a smarter tunic," I laughed, taking the waterskin from him.

"Oh, you look just fine as you are. Although I'm sure, given the work you are doing, you would be far more comfortable with no tunic on at all," he replied, his lips pulled into a crooked smile.

"It's very thoughtful of you to think of my comfort like that," I grinned.

"Just selflessly looking out for you, Rook," he replied, leaning his back against the wall and casting his eyes over me. "Are you taking a break?"

"Not just yet, I need to put these bundles out in the courtyard to dry. There are some useful herbs in here so I want to check with Evan where they can be stored."

"Do you want some help to move them? I wouldn't mind stretching my legs after sitting in the workshop all morning."

"If you think you can carry them," I teased.

"Well, I'll just have to show you won't I?" he replied, in a mocking tone.

"Go for it," I said, folding my arms and leaning my back against the cool stone wall, grinning at the determination in his face.

Barden hitched up the waist of his breeches and eyed the nearest bundle, before craning over and attempting to wrap his arms around it.

"Ah, the stalks... Ah... they keep stabbing me! How the hell am I meant to get my arms around this thing!?"

Chuckling, I pushed off the wall and stepped up next to him, leaning in, my face close to his. "Try the handle, handsome," I murmured, rolling the bundle to expose the loop of rope I had tied into the strand lashing it together.

He turned to me, our faces close. "Smart ass," he muttered, "did you make me struggle just so you could check out my ass?"

Laughing, I clapped him on the back and handed him a pair of gloves. I pulled on my own and grabbed the handle of the bundle and strode to the next bundle to pick that one up too. Lifting them both, I headed down the path, glancing behind me when I neared the courtyard archway to see Barden red-faced, half-carrying, half-dragging a bundle along the path. Dropping my load, I went over to help him.

"How...did you...carry two!?" he puffed

"Doing it every year since I can remember helps," Taking the bundle from him, noting Barden's eyes roaming my arms and chest as I lifted the bundle, I stacked it next to the others.

"Would I be guessing correctly that I will be moving the rest of these by myself?" I asked, raising my eyebrows at him.

Pausing a moment and glancing back over the rest of the bundles, he said "Gerard's breeches are very much in need of my urgent attention."

"Mhm, of course," I laughed.

After finding Evan in the kitchen to check where he wanted the bundles to be stored, I got back to work clearing another row. With no shade to offer me any relief from the heightening sun, I was soon sweating from the effort of swinging the scythe. Halfway along the row, I paused to catch my breath and remembering what Barden had said, glanced up to the second-story window of the weaver barn. The window was empty but open. Smirking, I removed my belt, throwing it aside then pulled off my tunic, discarding that too and got back to work. Just as I was tying off another bundle, Barden's voice called out to me, "Well, now. Isn't that more comfortable?"

His elbows were resting on the window frame, his black hair had fallen over his face, partially obscuring his eyes but his heated expression was still clear. Flashing him a smile, I set to with the scythe again. Knowing he was watching and admitting to myself that I wanted to impress him, even just a little bit, I put more effort into each swing feeling the pull in the muscles through my arms and back. Having only gone a short distance, curiosity to see if he was still watching got the better of me and I looked back up to the window.

He was still there.

He looked me over a moment longer before standing, running his hand through his hair, winking at me, and then disappearing into the workshop. With a broad grin plastered across my face, I continued with my work.

Chapter 12
Enchantress

The exchange between them tastes so sweet.

His body cuts an impressive line. His muscles bunch and release with the effort of his task and his strong grip and wide stance commands the scythe to his will. He puts such effort into all he does, taking long sweeping swings, cutting low to the earth to claim as much of the stalk as he can, to then carefully and meticulously bundle his prize.

Intrigued by his fascination, I watch as he notices a mouse jump from the grass just beyond his blade. There are not many who would track the journey of a small field mouse so intently and yet he pauses to follow the creature he disturbed until he becomes aware of my presence. He fumbles for a moment, an endearing trait, before dropping the scythe and moving towards me, turning into the sun, sweat gleaming across his bare chest. As he approaches, he attempts to keep his eyes down in what I would gather to be a show of respect, but he also can't seem to help himself from stealing glances at me.

"Good morning, Mistress. Such an honour to see you." He clasped his hands behind his back, his chest thrusting out beautifully.

"I have been watching you, Rook. You could have just cut the plants and then left them to die back but you saw the value in them and took the time to put them aside. You show an attentiveness for such seemingly small things that may otherwise go unnoticed. I am impressed by your level of care."

His face reddened but a small smile played on his lips, "High praise coming from you, Mistress. Thank you."

Chapter 13
Rook

A week's worth of continual effort saw half the paddock flora cut and bundled. Bolstered by the Enchantress' praise and determined to prove my devotion to my duties and her, I started each day at first light, often being the first person in the kitchen each morning, and continuing into the evening, making the most of the cooling hours as the last light faded.

One morning, I was storing the last of the dried-out bundles in the crop barn when Grace appeared, a bright smile on her face.

"Morning, Rook. I missed you at breakfast."

She wore a linen tunic, similar to those worn by the men only thinner and knee length, with snug-fitting leggings underneath, both already covered in a dusting of soil. The top half of her yellow hair was braided, odd strands coming loose here and there from a morning's work, while the rest fell over her shoulders. Coupled with the smudge of dirt across her nose and the blush on her cheeks I couldn't help but take her in.

Here's a sweet, pretty girl who wasn't afraid of hard work and looked damned cute while she was at it.

"Morning, Grace. I wanted to get all these bundles stored by midday before I started cutting the rest of the paddock."

Her gaze lingered long enough that I couldn't help but smirk. To my delight, she reciprocated with a blush. "Well, uhm, I was going to ask you..." she stammered, "I was wondering if you would like to come with me to put an offering at the forest shrine?"

The customs of providing offerings to the Enchantress varied across Marieena but wasn't something I had considered at the castle. "I didn't realise you put out offerings to the Enchantress here too"

She frowned, confusion spreading over her face. "Uhm, no, no, this is the offering for the Gods."

"An offering for the Gods?" Now it was my turn to be confused.

"Of course," she frowned slightly, "Do you not make offerings to the Gods at your shrine back home?"

I shrugged, feeling awkward. "Uhm, no. We send offerings and prayers to the Enchantress but the Gods are just tales...aren't they?"

She raised her eyebrows and smiled. "Depends what you believe," she replied.

"I didn't think they held much truth. Mother would tell me stories of the Sky Father and Mother Earth and their children but I didn't think they were true and even if they were, I never imagined they would care if I made offerings to them or not. I'm just one man."

"The Gods care greatly, Rook," she replied. "Our offerings show our praise and thanks to them for everything they give us. They dedicate their time and power to taking care of all things. We should at least thank them for it, don't you think?"

"Uhm, yeah, sure. I guess."

She narrowed her eyes at me, clearly not wholly convinced by my admission. "How about you come with me and make your own offering? Just in case they are watching. Can't hurt right?" The smirk plastered across her face made me laugh.

Can't fault her effort.

"Sure. Can't hurt."

Even if the Gods were any more than just tales, what notice would they take of the meagre offering I could provide? I was just a humble farmer, a happy and willing servant of the land. What care would they have for me?

"Great, give me an hour to gather what we need and meet me back here," she said.

"Perfect, I should be done storing the rest of the bundles by then."

When the final bundles were stacked in the crop store, I paused, leaning my back against the door frame and casting my eyes over the meadow. The spectacular array of colourful flowers stood tall, humming with the activity of insects. These were the kinds of days I lived for, and here they just seemed all the more perfect.

This could be home.

Home.

Harth.

A pang of sadness washed over me to think of my village. The noise and excitement of market day, the children paddling in the stream that trickled through the orchard, the spring flowers in the big field behind the shrine where we held the harvest festival every year.

If only all could be perfect there too.

Glancing at a lone tree across the meadow, my eyes snagged on a figure sitting just beyond its branches' shade. The Enchantress sat, knees to her chest, quietly watching me.

Eager for any time in my Mistress' company, particularly if that time was alone with her, I tentatively approached her. She looked so beautiful with the sun washing over her, its light sending rivers of shine through her hair. With her eyes closed and brow smooth, her upturned face looked pensive, as if contemplating something. Stopping a respectful distance away, I gently whispered to her, "Mistress."

"Don't be shy, my darling. Come and sit beside me."

Taking her outstretched hand in mine, I sat beside her, stealing glances at her as she continued to bask in the sun. What I would have given to know what she thought about, to get a glimpse into her mind and its workings. Did she know why the land was struggling? She surely knew these things were happening, but did she know why? It seemed impertinent to ask, but who else would know the answer if not her?

"I can hear your brain thinking," she smiled. "Is there something you would like to say?"

"Well, I was just thinking about the... the trees, and the crops, too." I glanced at her again, assessing her face before slowly continuing, "They don't seem to be... doing so well." She gave me no response, but since I had already started down this line of thought, I pushed on. "Why is this happening? Do you know what can be done?"

She stayed still for the longest time, and I grew concerned that she would not answer or that I had angered her with my line of questioning. Just as I was about to open my mouth to backtrack, she sighed, opened her eyes and looked out over the meadow.

"The sun, the earth and the water give life to everything," she began. "They do this dutifully and selflessly, and all they hope for in return is the love and devotion of the people they care for. Somehow, there are those who have forgotten this." She paused, swallowing hard. "They do not show their love and appreciation, but despite this, day after day, year after year, the Gods go on, giving their life force to maintain a world that has forgotten them." Her dejected tone pulled at my heart. "The old Gods have been forgotten... and I with them." She lowered her head, her face forlorn.

"Mistress," I breathed, distraught but not knowing how to comfort her. Her words hung in the air, heavy in their sadness. Guilt for not only my own ignorance but that of those I had grown up with, flooded me. What could I say to make this better? The truth was surely the best thing but I didn't want to highlight my ignorance to her, but what choice did I have? "I admit that I did not consider the land, the river or the sun to be any more than what they appear to be, but the tales of the old Gods are just that aren't they? Tales?"

She must have sensed the desperation in my voice as when she turned back to me her face was full of sympathy. "It's alright, Rook. I know it is a lot to consider." She ran her hand through my hair, comforting me. "The Gods inhabit everything around us. The sun, the land, the water, yes, but also the little things; the forest grove intended for lovers, the quiet of the night where the crickets sing, the music that has the magic to lift our soul. The old Gods care for the smaller parts of the world that are less considered which is why they have been so easily forgotten."

"But you could never be forgotten, Mistress," I pressed. "How could you? You have always been here, protecting us. I will admit I don't know how your magic works but I know that those times back home when all seemed lost, when the rain came just as we needed it, when the harvest was set to ruin, it was you that saved us."

"You give me far more credit than is due," she replied. "There are many that would be worthy of your praise, some of which are no longer with us. The land suffers without its guardians to protect it... as I suffer without them too. I am all but alone and being forgotten. My magic is... fading because no one believes anymore."

Guardians?

"I will do all I can to protect you, Mistress. I will make people see!" I cried, my voice rising. "You are a wonder! Even the Gods themselves must delight in you!"

Frowning slightly and regarding me for a moment with a curious expression, she asked, "What do you consider me to be, Rook?"

"I... uh... confess my ignorance, Mistress." Embarrassed again to be showing the level of my ignorance to her, I sought to make up for it with my adoration for her. "To me, when faced with the question of what you are, my mind considers only the beauty that you are and that which you create. Where it all comes from, beyond you, is of little importance to me."

"Rook, my darling, I need to show you something."

The Enchantress led me through to the East paddock where I had partially cleared the long grasses. She stopped beside a lone sapling, her face clouded with sadness as she stared at it. "My magic isn't endless and it is weakening. There is so much more I wish I could give. To the land, to the water, to everyone." She squeezed her eyes closed tightly for a moment before turning to look at me. "I give what I can but it isn't enough anymore. Let me show you."

She knelt on the bare earth and placed her hands on the ground at the young tree's base, closing her eyes and furrowing her brow in concentration. For a few moments, nothing appeared to happen. Seemingly undeterred, the Enchantress remained at her station while I looked on, determined not to blink in case I should miss something. Concern crept through me as her fingers dug into the earth and her hands and arms trembled with the effort she expelled to what appeared to be no effect.

Just as it crossed my mind to go to her, small green buds suddenly appeared on the lengthening branches of the sapling, becoming bigger as I watched and eventually unfolding into fresh, new leaves. Every branch grew thicker, longer, reaching high, the cracking of its expanding bark sounding like a fanfare as it spread its foliage in triumph.

Letting out a gasp, her eyes flew open. She drew back, breathing heavily and turned to me, delight spread over her face. I had never witnessed anything more magnificent. In utter awe and on shaking legs, I slipped to my knees, mouth gaping, unable to do anything but stare at her, her slightly flushed face alive with pride but tinged with sadness. "It's only one tree, but it's one more tree," she smiled.

My eyes travelled the length of the stout trunk of the tree before us, which now stood twice my height. Biased I may be to my Mistress' magic, but this tree was the most magnificent I had ever seen. It was luminous in its colour, lit as if from within rather than just the sun shining upon it. And it appeared to stand prouder, its stance one of strength and triumph. I looked back to my Mistress still kneeling beside the tree and had to swallow hard to clear my throat. "Mistress, you are beyond this world."

She cast her eyes down for a moment before looking at me, her eyes shining with tears, "I am in awe of your devotion, Rook. The Gods may only have been tales to you but your unwavering sense of duty to me has never failed." She paused, the sadness returning. "You do so much but... without my Alpha I don't know what the future holds. But know this, I see your care and appreciation, and it fills me with love."

Alpha? So... they are real?

If that's the case, where the hell are they?

I crawled a little closer to her, desperate to show her she wasn't alone. "It isn't hard to love you, Mistress, or devote myself to you and your cause. I love what you are... I love what you give and... I love you." Feeling my face flush I looked away so as not to let her see my embarrassment at such an admission.

"Sweet boy. I know, darling. I can feel your love and it is all I will ever ask of you. That and maybe another one of those pretty straw hearts."

My head whipped around to look at her. Her smile spread wide as she squeezed my hand.

I had no idea she actually received those.

Bringing her hand to my lips, I kissed it and returned her smile. "You shall have a thousand."

Chapter 15
Rook

The late afternoon sun was just above the trees when I noticed Grace waiting at the entrance to the meadow. Our Mistress kissed her cheek as she passed her leaving a pink tinge on her face. Grace watched her leave before turning to me. "You can take those to the forest shrine as your offering to the Gods," she said, gesturing to two sheaves of barley straw leaning up against the wall. "It is customary for farmers to offer some of what is left of their winter stores in the spring, as thanks for a safe winter."

"Perfect, thank you."

I must be sure to set some aside to weave.

"You're welcome. Shall we go?" Grace carried a basket of root vegetables while I slung a sheaf under each arm. "The shrine isn't far."

She led me out of the meadow, through the courtyard beyond, and into the forest. The leaves swayed in a gentle breeze, the sunlight sifting through them creating mottled figures through the trees that kept themselves just out of reach but teased us along the path nonetheless. I shifted the bundles under my arm to a more secure position and strode on after them and Grace.

I wonder if the Gods would be watching us now.

Glancing around as if I might see one of them and wondering what exactly I would see if I did, I hoped they would be satisfied with what I carried. Even if I wasn't certain they were actually there or cared about me or any offering I put forth, if there was a chance they were paying attention, I didn't want to offend them. Mistress had painted such a sad picture of the ongoing, devoted service that the Gods provided, despite so many humans being ungrateful for it. I was adamant not to be seen as one of those humans. Our Mistress seemed pleased by my efforts, and I hoped this would go some way to please the Gods too.

"You are very quiet, Rook. Anything on your mind?" Grace's voice shook me out of my wonderings.

"I was just hoping this will be enough," I replied.

"It isn't the size of the offering that's important. It's the intention to give thanks that is noticed. They enjoy being part of our lives. They watch us from afar, but have also been known to walk among us." She spoke quickly, her eyes bright and wide, revelling in her storytelling. "Some show themselves to humans so they can interact with us. Some even appear as humans, so you wouldn't know they were a God."

Considering her words for a moment, I asked, "Like the Alphas?"

"You would have to ask Gerard about Alphas. I don't know much about them. But whatever they are, God, human or something else entirely, they are not around anymore and were rarely seen when they were. But I do know this, they were said to be relentless in their pursuit of their mates but no one really knows what happened to them."

Jealousy ravaged my mind at the idea of someone coming and taking our Mistress from us, from me.

No one is worthy of her.

Least of all someone who has neglected their duty to protect her.

Fists clenched, I tried to calm myself and not dwell on the possibility of this happening. As Grace said, Alphas were gone. Our Mistress wasn't going anywhere and we would do what we could to help her now.

"Here we are." Grace stopped in a small clearing. A large mound with an arched entrance stood next to a pine tree so tall I couldn't see the top. "We come here for the new moon ceremony which is held in the shrine chamber through there. We leave the offerings for the Gods over here though."

Following her past the entrance to the shrine, I craned to look through the archway to see into the chamber but could only see a dark tunnel leading steadily downwards. Grace knelt at the base of the pine near a small hollow in the tree's trunk. "This is one of the oldest trees in the forest. Mistress speaks highly of it, as you might an old friend."

There were trees back home that I had spent many years visiting again and again. Season after season, I had watched them bloom through the warm months and then quietly shed their leaves before the winter storms. Their presence shaped the land, providing landmarks for generations, their trunks offering a stout resting post for any weary or lonely soul. They stood, ever waiting, standing strong in the face of all but the harshest hardships, for me to rest my back upon them in a loving familiarity. Looking up at this glorious old tree and thinking back on those I had spent my time with, I could see why the Enchantress would consider them old friends. There was an imposing nature to this stout old pine. The other trees around it seemed to stand clear as if to show respect. A rustle through its branches as Grace laid down her offering could almost have been mistaken for a voice, rough and textured as a wood flute.

Once she was done carefully arranging our offerings, Grace moved to sit by the stream, patting a rock to invite me to sit next to her as she placed her feet in the water. She ran her hand through the water, cupping it and letting it fall through her fingers.

"Sometimes I think I can almost feel Mistress' magic," she said, her eyes fixed on the drips running down her arm. Slowly, she slid her fingers over her cheek, a small smile coming over her face as the water left glittering trails across her skin.

"Really?"

"Hmm. After each ceremony, the water always seems different somehow, shinier, and the smells of the forest are stronger."

Tentatively, I breathed deeper, trying to pull more air through my nose in an attempt to feel what Grace did. To me, the forest smelled as it always had but then this was a new place to me and I was not yet familiar with its secrets.

"Look!" Grace whispered.

Turning to where she eagerly gestured, I noticed a hare slowly making its way out of the bushes towards the offerings we had left under the tree.

"Huh, it's been a while since..."

"Shhh!" Grace urged, putting her hand on my arm.

We watched as it plucked several strands of straw from one of the bundles before disappearing back into the undergrowth.

"An offering accepted by a disguised God or a mother building her nest?" Grace said, cocking her head to the side as she giggled, her face bright with a keen smile.

Sweet girl.

We were on our way back to the castle when glancing over Grace's shoulders, I saw Brianna coming through the forest towards us. Her red hair was pulled into a tight braid that ran from the top of her head and hung to her waist. She had foliage stuck to her fur cape and breeches, and her face was smeared with what looked like mud but I couldn't be certain. Just as I was about to hail her, she placed a finger to her lips in a gesture of 'be quiet'. Silently, she snuck up behind Grace and stepping up behind her, wrapped an arm around her waist and pressed her lips to her neck. Grace's breath hitched but she relaxed into the embrace.

Brianna nipped at her ear. "Mmm, what a tasty morsel."

"Ahh!" Grace exclaimed, in mock protest, giggling as she squealed, "Save me, Rook!"

"You know, I would, but honestly, I think Brianna could take me," I laughed, folding my arms to watch the scene unfold.

Both women laughed. Grace twirled around in Brianna's grip so she was facing her, wrapped her arms around her neck and kissed her. "Welcome home, Brie. Missed you."

"Missed you too, little flower," Brianna replied, a loving smile spreading over her face as she leaned to kiss Grace again. "I caught a brace of rabbits. We can ask Evan to make your favourite."

"Mmm, yum. You spoil me."

"Always," Brianna replied, giving Grace a tight squeeze before letting her go. "I also put an old doe out of her misery. She was stumbling around the forest, looked like her hips had given up on her. Poor ol' gal. Be a good lad would you Rook and give me a hand with her? I put her down just by that blackberry bush over there." Brianna pointed into the trees to a small thicket where the sun made it to the forest floor.

"Of course." Heading to where Brianna had gestured, I was surprised at the size of the deer lying peacefully on the ground, a small wound in its chest where Brianna's expertly shot arrow would have hit its heart.

Impressive.

Taking hold of the deer's legs, I heaved it up and onto my shoulders, its soft fur rubbing against my neck as I followed the women back to the castle.

Considering the possibility that out there in the forest somewhere was a God that wept for the old doe, I carried her carefully, quietly thanking them for her.

As we passed through the courtyard, Grace looked in on the East paddock.

"Looks good in here, Rook. Just one left to go?" She nodded to the Enchantress' tree.

"Uh, no actually. I'm keeping that one."

"Oh? Why on earth would you keep a tree in the middle of a crop paddock? That's going to make things difficult isn't it?"

"It might. But it's staying." I looked out over the paddock with its lone tree proudly taking centre stage, firm in my resolution to keep it there.

"When the Mistress makes a special effort to make something grow before your very eyes, you don't dishonour her by tearing it down. You cherish it."

A hand landed on my arm, quickly followed by Grace's head pressing against me. "You are the sweetest man I know, Rook. I'm so happy you are here."

Warmed by her words, I tilted my head to rest it on top of hers.

Chapter 16
Enchantress

Y ou cherish it...

Is there no end to this man's devotion?

Stepping into the light, I watched Grace and Brianna leave together while Rook hesitated.

"There is so much more here than I ever expected," he muttered to himself.

Gently running a hand over the fur of the old doe he held over his shoulder, he turned and saw me, pausing a moment before greeting me.

"Mistress." He inclined his head to me as best he could with the doe over his shoulders.

"I saw you in the forest," I admitted. "I heard your thanks. You honour the Gods with your offering and tenderness."

I couldn't resist running my hand over his handsome face, his skin smooth and warm against my fingers.

"I would welcome you in my chamber tonight," I whispered, relishing the change in his expression.

Chapter 17

Rook

"This is it," Grace said, knocking on the door, a knowing smirk spreading across her face that left me feeling uneasy. "Don't be nervous. You're perfect and Mistress must think so too to invite you to her chamber." Kissing me on the cheek, she pushed open one of the doors. I took a deep breath and stepped inside.

The large room beyond had tall ceilings and intricate hangings covering the walls, depicting different forest scenes in exceptional detail woven from delicate threads. An immense fireplace filled the wall to my left, a crackling fire snapping in the grate with a large fur rug on the floor in front of it. A decadent four-poster bed sat on my right with thick, smoothly carved posts in each corner and a canopy of a deep shade of green. Before me, a sofa with a heavy fur thrown over it, on which lounged the Enchantress. The slip dress she wore clung to every curve of her beautiful body and rode high on her thighs, exposing her smooth legs. Her arm rested on her slender waist, delicate fingers toying with the fabric of her dress.

"Good evening," she purred, slowly sliding her legs off the sofa to sit upright, giving me a glimpse, as she did, of the downy hair between her thighs. "You have pleased me, Rook."

"Thank you, Mistress," I stammered, sweating and shifting my weight, my body suddenly feeling awkward and thick. My physical response to her was instantaneous and embarrassingly out of my control, which unnerved me.

"You have been here a little while now. Do you still wish to stay and serve me?" she asked, her eyes glowing.

"Yes, Mistress," I clamped my sweaty hands behind my back, feeling awkward, not knowing what else to do with them, but too late, realising this left the bulge in the front of my breeches more obvious. Conflicted, I unclasped my hands only to clasp them again, not wanting to draw attention to the situation by moving them in front of me, all the while painfully aware the Enchantress was watching me.

She grinned, her eyes hooded. "And you know what it means to serve me?" She ran her fingers slowly up her bare thigh.

I tracked the path of her hand, blinking hard, and then looked up to the ceiling, trying to focus. I shifted my weight nervously from one foot to the other, trying to make my mind work so I could respond.

"I have...some idea, Mistress," my voice caught in a desperate whisper as my desire boiled close to the surface. I looked back at her, hoping the invitation to spend the evening with her meant that she wanted me to stay at the castle too.

"Mmm," she sighed, her hand sliding back down her thigh. "Your service here would require complete devotion of yourself, Rook. Will you devote yourself to me, all of yourself?" she asked

My lips were bone dry and I had to lick them so I could answer. "Yes, Mistress. You have been in my thoughts...well, always. I have longed to serve you and have no greater desire than to give myself to you." I was relieved to have gotten any words out but couldn't seem to stop my fidgeting. With her eyes on me, my body was not my own.

"Such pretty words, my darling," she said, "and now I want you to prove it."

My stomach lurched.

Oh hell. This is it.

"Anything for you, Mistress." I managed to stutter, "Just tell me what you want of me."

I watched her tongue slide out of the corner of her upturned mouth and pause on her lip for a moment.

"Come here."

On shaky legs, I crossed the room to stand in front of her. Heat seemed to radiate from her, making my skin flare and sweat bloom across my body. My senses were so overtaken by her that my mind was utterly blank.

"I want you to take off your breeches so I can see all of you," she said, sliding her hips back on the sofa and leaning forward to rest her elbows on her thighs. She ran her index finger along her lower lip, raising her chin slightly with an intense interest in her expression.

I paused for a moment to take in what she had said, then gathering myself, replied, "Yes, Mistress."

The thought of being naked with this divine woman was making my breeches uncomfortable, but this wasn't like any coupling I had taken part in before. It was with her, the Enchantress I had yearned for, the one I had cherished in my mind for so long that suddenly I was concerned my body would disappoint her. Would my mere mortal body be enough to please her the way I wanted it to?

With my breath shallow and my body tense with anticipation, I forced my trembling fingers to undo the laces of my breeches and slid them slowly down my thighs. Despite my nerves, my cock stood firmly erect and instantly sprang free. Stepping out of my breeches, my face burned with embarrassment. Not knowing what else to do with them, I clasped my hands behind my back again, looked up to the ceiling and slowly breathed out to calm myself.

There was a moment's silence. I gradually lowered my gaze to look at her. The tip of her thumb was now between her teeth as she stared at my erect cock. Slowly her eyes slid to mine and she smiled.

"Attentive, aren't you? Good boy," she whispered, her eyes ablaze.

I smiled nervously, surprised by the bolt of pleasure that shot through me at her praise.

I waited with bated breath for her to speak again.

"Now, I want you to come here and kneel in front of me. Put your knees on either side of my leg."

Encouraged by her approval, I hastened to do as she asked and shot forward. I felt self-conscious as I came close to her, but relished the intimacy. I knelt, carefully putting a knee on either side of her foot, trying not to touch her with my straining cock. Her legs were parted, and I tried hard not to stare at her bare thighs.

"Put your chin on my hand and keep your eyes on me," she said, reaching her upturned palm forward.

Curious where this was going, I leaned my chest and chin uncomfortably forward to reach her hand and looked up into her eyes. Her face was even more beautiful this close-up. She had a light spattering of freckles across the bridge of her nose that I found very endearing. Her skin was velvety soft against my jaw and smelled sweet like spring flowers. She had a warm look on her face that put me a little at ease. She smiled, and

I smiled back. As she stroked my cheek with her thumb, I closed my eyes for a moment, enjoying her touch, before opening them again.

"Sweet boy," she leaned forward to look deeper into my eyes. My eyes flicked from one to another, feeling their fiery, penetrating gaze and felt a rush of heat through my body again, which had my cock bobbing only inches from her leg.

"Now, Rook, my darling, you are going to take that attentive cock of yours and rub it against my leg until you spill your seed, and you are going to keep your eyes on me the whole time."

My eyes widened. That was not what I had expected her to say. I froze, mind blank, my eyes boring into hers, not knowing what to do. She continued to look at me, and a moment later, she said, "Darling Rook, don't you want to gift your Mistress your seed?"

I rubbed the roof of my mouth with my tongue and swallowed hard. "Of course, Mistress."

I wasn't the most experienced man when it came to sex. The lack of women I found attractive in Harth had seen to that, but what she asked of me was not something I had ever heard my brothers talk about either. The stories they shared were about the women sucking their shaft or sitting on their bare laps, but never anything like this. Sure, I had given myself relief before, but never in this manner. It was a solitary affair born of necessity and frustration with little sensuality, not for the desire of another. But I wanted to please her, and if this was what would please her...

Slowly I moved my knees closer to her, my arms at my sides to balance myself and I brought my hips forward. The tip of my cock made contact with her smooth leg, and I closed my eyes and groaned, enjoying her cool, silky flesh.

"Keep your eyes open," she ordered.

My eyes snapped open immediately, locking with hers. "Yes, Mistress." The words fell out of my mouth in a hurry to obey her.

Staring into those fierce green eyes, I started to rock my hips back and forth, rubbing the head of my shaft against her leg. She smiled at me, a playful grin that sent tingles through my groin. I felt self-conscious looking into her eyes while I rubbed my ever-stiffening cock against her leg, but my hips moved of their own accord, leaving me unable to stop them. For a moment, I thought about the horny farm dog we had once had back home who would hump the leg of my eldest brother and felt my face redden. Was this what I was to her? A horny dog that was here to obey her but was allowed my relief at her whim? I hadn't expected it to, but this thought drove me mad with lust.

I groaned as I began to leak, lubricating her smooth leg, allowing me to slide more easily up and down it. My pace increased again, and as the pleasure began to build, I grunted and reached my hands forward to clasp her thigh to steady myself.

"That's it," she urged, crooning to me in a breathy, eager voice.

Delighted to hear the passion in her voice, I groaned again, my hips snapping back and forth as the frantic need to please her took over me. Her eyes were fixed on mine as I struggled to keep my eyes open as the pleasure mounted.

"Show me your devotion, Rook," she whispered.

My balls tightened, and I gritted my teeth as I felt my climax coming. Pleasure surged through my body. My grip on her leg tightened, and I squeezed my eyes closed for a moment. I let out a low growl and gritted my teeth harder as my seed burst over her leg. When I looked into her eyes again, they seemed to shine as they bore into me. I felt exposed to her, laid bare in this vulnerable moment of climax, as my body shuddered and my breath came in ragged gasps.

My hips snapped a couple more times as my cock released its full load, relief and pleasure running in waves through my body. The Enchantress leaned forward and pressed her lips to mine as my hips twitched out the last of my ejaculation. This took me by surprise, but I quickly pushed my lips against hers, breathed in her sweet scent, and let out a deep sigh. Sliding her leg between mine, she leaned back and gently directed my head to her lap. I eagerly pressed my face against her warm, bare thighs, wrapping my arms around her hips and breathed in her smell.

Hers was the most intoxicating scent I had ever encountered. I took deep, long breaths through my nose as my cock gently bobbed against her leg. Her scent made me think of the fresh spring mornings when the dew hadn't quite disappeared and the world was quiet, gentle and at peace. My mind wandered to the smell of the trees after the autumn rains when the air was damp and fresh. She stroked my hair as I rested my head in her lap and in response I placed a gentle kiss on her thigh, letting out a deep sigh, feeling utterly content.

Chapter 18
Enchantress

When this one blushes...

He is like no one else.

His offering overwhelms me, stuttering my breath with its potent presence.

Chapter 19
Rook

Pushing hard against the handle, I freed the blade of my pick axe from the ground, finally uprooting the stubborn shrub.

That was not what I had expected at all. Just thinking back over what had happened in the Enchantress' chamber the evening before had me feeling hot and doubling my fruitless efforts to distract myself with work. I had never been so orchestrated in a sexual act before. She knew exactly what she wanted of me and that I would give it to her, longed to give it to her, despite the way it made me feel like her needy pet.

Don't complain, you know you loved it.

I couldn't deny it to myself that I really had enjoyed every moment of it. Still, I had been a well-respected member of my village back home. A strong man who was his own master, looked up to for my years of dedication to my duty and knowledge of my craft. Was it acceptable that I should enjoy such a submissive role in a coupling? Even if it was to our Enchantress? I slammed the pick axe into the ground again, trying to concentrate on uprooting the tree I had set as my task to putting these thoughts from my mind for a while.

"How are you, Rook?" Gerard's sudden appearance caught me off guard. "Sorry, boy. Didn't mean to startle you. I did call out." Seeming to sense my unrest, he stepped close to me and put his hand on my shoulder. "Why don't you take a break? Come talk to me." Guiding me to the wall, he sat down beside me and after rummaging in his pocket, handed me an apple, which I gratefully accepted.

We sat in silence for a while, Gerard crunching his apple, looking out over the paddock seemingly at nothing, but I could feel him waiting for me. Having glanced several times at him, his face calm and patient, and realising he wasn't going to be the one to break the silence, I decided to broach the subject on my mind.

"So, I spent the evening with Mistress."

"An honour indeed." His face remained placid, a gentle smile curving his lips, while he maintained his steady, distant gaze, which I appreciated. I fumbled through the thoughts in my mind as I tried to put them into words.

"It was... nothing like I have experienced before."

"I see." He threw his apple core into the long grass. "Did you enjoy yourself?"

"Very much, but..." I halted, not knowing how to continue or even whether Gerard would want to know such intimate thoughts. The silence stretched out a moment. Taking the opportunity my pause presented, Gerard settled back on one elbow, stretching his long legs out in front of him. Gently he offered, "You know, Rook, there are things in life that don't require explanation. Our pleasures, for example. Whatever they are, are ours to keep and share with only those we wish to." He paused, allowing me time to consider his words.

"It's just, I have never thought myself a... weak man," I ventured, furrowing my brow, trying to find a way to explain myself.

"And why would you? You are strong, capable and smart. There is no reason why you would think that of yourself, is there?"

"But last night..."

"Doesn't change you as the person you are, just maybe opened your eyes to other pleasures," he said, turning to look at me. "Is it weakness to satisfy your pleasure? Is it weakness to love our Mistress? I don't think so, but it is you who must come to accept this."

Nodding my response, I took a bite of my apple and cast my mind again to the Enchantress' chamber, reliving its intensity so vividly that I felt my body swell. Interpreting my fidgeting for uncertainty, Gerard changed the subject, "How about coming to meet the horses tomorrow morning?"

Relieved for the distraction, I nodded. Patting me on the shoulder, Gerard stood, "Great, I'll see you at first light. And Rook, you seek me out if you need to, alright?"

"Thanks, Gerard."

"You're welcome, boy. Tomorrow then," he said and left.

Chapter 20

Rook

The strong smell of barley straw, horses and leather greeted me as I pushed through the large double wooden doors into the horse barn the next morning. The vast building had an impressive skeleton of stout wooden beams which made up the high ceiling. The stone walls looked thick enough to withstand the harshest storms.

"Morning Rook. Ahh, smells good doesn't it?" Gerard was chipper and covered in straw despite the early hour. He took a deep breath in, making a point of his enjoyment of his surroundings. "Tristan complains that I make the library smell of horse."

Imagining Tristan flapping a book at Gerard to shoo him out of the library made me chuckle.

"Sun's nearly up, and the horses will be eager for their breakfast. This way."

Gerard disappeared into a small room beside the barn doors for a moment, returning with a leather head collar which he handed to me. I turned it over in my hands, admiring the craftsmanship that had gone into it.

"This is beautiful. The leather is so soft and supple, and the engravings are very intricate."

"Thank you," Gerard beamed, glancing at the collar in my hands. "I made it myself. I had little time back home for leather work, but I have far fewer horses to care for here, so I have time for other things. It took a while to make, but I enjoyed it, and it was worth the effort." His smile gave his pride for the piece away.

"It's impressive work. I'd love to turn my hand to something so skilled."

"I'd be happy to show you how I made it the next time I have the chance to make another if you like?" The eagerness in his voice to invite me to share in his interests flattered me.

"Really? I'd love to see that."

Gerard's effort to distract me with his gentle manner and kind offer didn't go unnoticed. I was grateful to him. I was still finding my place and figuring out what it was to serve here and his guidance put me at ease.

"Sure thing, boy." He wrapped his arm around my shoulder in a friendly embrace and steered me across the barn. "Come on, let's get these horses."

Striding through the thick straw bed of the barn, leather boots wrapped tight around his calves, red hair falling in loose waves over his summer tunic, he looked every bit the calm horse master. The freckles spattered over his face and creases around his eyes hinted at the years spent working outside in the sun.

Emerging from the barn, a vast, rolling pasture spread before us, framed by tall trees on either side with a backdrop of heather-covered mountains. The knee-deep swathes of meadow grasses bent and swayed in the light, early morning breeze.

"Where are the horses?" I asked.

Gerard, grinning at me, turned out to the seemingly empty pasture. He raised his hands to his face, cupped his mouth, took a deep breath and let out a long, high-pitched herding song that echoed across the whole valley. He paused for a moment, letting the echo die away before taking another breath and calling out more notes. His voice was eerie but beautiful. He paused once again, and in his silence, a distant whinny answered him.

"There they are," he said, turning back to me.

I scanned the pasture, waiting. A low rumbling sound, which steadily grew louder, followed the whinny. Distant pinpricks appeared on the mound, which turned into the majestic bodies of nine horses. Long manes streamed around them as they galloped towards us, tossing their heads. They were stunning creatures, power and grace personified in muscular flesh. Our old plough horse back home was a handsome old boy, but he had nothing on these beauties.

They bucked and snorted as they maintained their incredible pace across the pasture, coming up on us fast. Gerard stepped ahead of me, raised his hands out in front of him, palms to the horses, and waited. Concern was rising in me as the horses neared, but didn't slow their pace. I glanced nervously between the horses and Gerard. Thirty feet short of him, the horses finally tucked their hindquarters under and slid to a gentle trot, steadying to a walk behind a particularly chunky bay who, ahead of the rest, came gently forwards to place their nose in Gerard's palm.

"Bandaa, my sweet." Gerard leant down to place his cheek just above the horse's nostril and, closing his eyes, breathed with the horse. I watched, fascinated, as they stood quietly together, sharing breath, calm and still, with a look of great contentment. Another of the horses, a more slender black animal, slowly sidled up along Bandaa and reached out to tentatively rub their muzzle in Gerard's hair. Chuckling, Gerard looked up and reached a hand out, letting them place their nose in his palm.

"This charming mare is Bandaa," Gerard said, turning to me and gesturing to the bay.

"She was one of those who came with me here. Her sister, Met, is the slightly lighter bay behind her and this pretty girl is her daughter, Sheena." He rubbed the neck of the black mare insisting on his attention.

"The big grey, patiently waiting on his ladies, is Fawn. He is Sheena's father and one of my best foundation stallions. He's an old lad now though and I like to keep a close eye on him because our newcomer, young man Fret over there, gets a bit boisterous with him now he's coming into himself." Gerard gestured to a gangly pale grey horse who was nipping at Fawn's hind legs, warranting terse looks from the old stallion.

"The four huddled together way at the back are our latest arrivals from my stud back in Scaw. We are just getting to know each other."

I glanced over the backs of the others to see four youngsters, scrawny by comparison to the others, in a mixture of colours but all a similar height and with the standard butt-high conformation expected of such young horses.

"They won't do any physical work for quite some time. They will just follow the others and learn through watching. Building a relationship with them is the most important thing at this point. Maybe you could help me?"

Raising my brows, I couldn't help but laugh. "Horse master to the Enchantress of Marieena needs my help teaching the baby horses? Riiight."

Gerard glanced at me from the corner of his eyes, his smirk giving him away. "I don't know what you are talking about."

"Alright, alright," I replied, holding up my hands. "Whatever it is, I'm here for it."

Gerard's smirk widened, a knowing look passing over his face before he continued his lesson.

"You may think that it's the stallion whose trust is the most hard-earned in a herd, but it is the older mares who guide the herd and maintain order within, so they must be the most sceptical and hard-headed for it. Earning a horse's trust is of the utmost importance if you are going to ask them to work for you." He paused and gave me a poignant stare.

Gerard's expression and the hollow feeling in my stomach told me we were not just talking about the horses anymore. I waited, beginning to sweat a little, wondering exactly where he was going with this.

"Have you heard of the term 'collaring' before?" he asked.

I shook my head.

"It refers to the use of a collar to show subservience to another within a relationship of trust and mutual love."

Aaaaaand there it is.

"When my horses wear their collar, they offer me a position of authority where they will give themselves over to me if I offer them love, care and respect."

Respect for a subservient.

The lesson he planned on bestowing upon me was becoming clearer.

Gerard took hold of either side of the noseband of the collar and, taking a step back, knelt down and held open the noseband in front of him. Bandaa regarded him a moment, then, taking a quiet step forward, reached her nose down and into the collar. Gerard slowly slid the headpiece behind her ears and buckled it.

"The collar is willingly accepted as a sign of mutual trust and understanding. These horses are strong and fast; they could easily out-manoeuvre me or pull the rope from my hand should they wish to. But I have earned their trust, which allows them to feel safe in my hands." He rubbed Bandaa between the eyes and slowly stood up.

"It is a privilege when these animals offer us their trusting company; we must honour that." With an affectionate rub to Bandaa's ear, Gerard turned and headed back to the barn, the rest of the herd following behind.

Gerard led Bandaa through the open barn doors, the rest of the herd following behind. Removing Bandaa's head collar, Gerard scattered the scraps from a bucket around the barn for the herd to seek out. "It's an interesting game for them to play, and nothing goes to waste," Gerard said in explanation. "Come sit with me."

I had thought I had come here to help him with the horses so I was confused when we left them in the barn to climb the staircase to the hay store. The hay store was an open room with a rail around the edge so we could look down on the horses as they ambled about in the barn. Gerard pulled a bale closer to the rail, and we sat together, looking down on the horses, snuffling through the straw to find their apple cores and carrot tops.

Gerard busied himself lazily wrapping a piece of hay around his finger when he casually glanced over to me. "I have asked Tristan to join us."

Chapter 21
Rook

“Tristan? I didn't know he was interested in the horses.”

“He isn't,” Gerard replied, a sly grin on his face.

“Then why...?”

“You will see, boy.”

My stomach clenched at his words.

Footsteps announced Tristan's arrival, and Gerard patted the hay bale next to him for Tristan to settle himself.

“Hey there you two,” his gentle voice sang out as he sat between us. He leaned into Gerard who wrapped an arm around his shoulder, beaming down at him as their lips softly came together.

I glanced between them, enjoying their tender greeting while being all too aware of how close they were to me. Tristan's thigh rested close enough to mine that I could feel his body heat.

They made a beautiful pair. Tristan looked slender next to Gerard's broader and taller frame. His long sandy hair fell loose around his shoulders, which he tucked behind one of his slightly pointed ears, giving me full view of their lips meeting. His delicate frame and tidy appearance looked out of place in a hay loft. My eyes roamed over his chest, arms and long, slender fingers and noticed he held something in his hand. I couldn't quite see what it was, but Gerard gently took it from him as he embraced him.

Secluded setting.

No one else around.

Feels rather familiar...

Leaning to look at me, Gerard said, "Tristan is here to help me share something with you, Rook. If you could stand by the rail there please."

I moved to where he gestured. Turning to Tristan and kissing him again, he said, "Would you lie back on the bale please, my love?"

"Sure thing," Tristan's lyrical voice replied, an impish grin spreading across his face as he lay back along the hay bale, hair streaming over the edge.

Gerard opened his hand showing me a smooth, leather collar laid out across his palm.

"Remember what I said about the collar? It is a sign of submission but also trust. Tristan will submit to me but trusts me to take care of and be respectful of him, which is why we have a hand signal if he needs me to stop. Tristan."

Tristan raised one hand and made a vee with his fore and middle finger.

"If I see this signal, I stop whatever I'm doing." He leaned down and, taking Tristan's fingers in his hand, lovingly kissed the tip of each one before looking at me again. "Got it?"

I nodded, my breath shallow as my excitement and apprehension grew.

Tristan was the one who lay prone yet a simple hand gesture is all he needs to take control of Gerard.

Care and respect.

Tristan had a look that said he had no mind to make anything that was about to happen stop. Gerard held my gaze for a few moments before unbuckling the collar and holding it above Tristan. "May I?"

"Yes, Sir." Tristan bit his bottom lip and smiled up at Gerard, eagerly wiggling a little further up the hay bale towards him, a bulge already forming in the front of his breeches.

A dark smile spread across Gerard's face, making me sweat and suddenly unable to stand still.

Tristan raised his head so Gerard could slip the collar under his head and down to his neck, buckling it snuggly around his throat. I stood absolutely still, lips bone dry from breathing with an open mouth. The only reason I didn't feel as though I was intruding on a private moment was that Gerard had invited me here, and Tristan knew I was watching.

Unlike the night in the library...

Shut up! That was different.

"Is that OK, boy?" Gerard's voice was heavy, a thick air of authority about him.

"Yes, Sir," gasped Tristan, his hooded eyes fixed on Gerard.

"Excellent," Gerard muttered, his voice rough.

Gerard slid his fingers under the collar, brushing Tristan's throat, eliciting a moan from him before suddenly tugging hard on the collar to pull his head over the edge of the hay bale.

Fuck.

Tristan's answering moan heated my abdomen and roused my cock. I took a sharp breath, unable to help myself, feeling my heart beat faster. Gerard glanced at me from under his brows again, his eyes all heat, a grin on his face at my response. My chest swelled, and my anticipation and curiosity peaked. Looking back at Tristan, whose eyes had not left him, Gerard released his hold on the collar and slowly unlaced his breeches. My mouth was wide open as I stared unashamedly at these two beautiful men, eager for what was coming. Gerard's breeches hit the floor, his massive shaft fully erect, the head a deep red.

"Now," he drawled to Tristan, "I am going to slide my cock down that eager throat of yours, and you are going to swallow it until I come. Would you like that?"

Oh fuck.

"Very much, Sir," replied Tristan.

"Good boy."

Gerard stepped forward, placing his thighs on either side of Tristan's head and took hold of the collar around his neck with one hand. With the other, he braced against the hay bale beside Tristan's chest. Tristan opened his mouth wide and eagerly stuck his tongue out to meet the head of Gerard's now leaking cock. Gerard moaned as he rubbed the head of his cock up and down Tristan's tongue.

"Tristan," Gerard moaned, "I want you to touch yourself while I take your throat."

Tristan's hand scrambled to undo his laces and pulling his erection free, rubbed it vigorously as he lapped at Gerard's, his moans muffled around Gerard's tip.

They looked glorious. Both men strained; their bodies tight, muscles flexed as they gave themselves to each other. Gerard seemed to be trying to restrain himself, while Tristan arched his back against the bale trying to command the interaction. Collar held snugly in his hand, Gerard's hips began to grind, slowly pushing himself in and out of Tristan's mouth.

Gods, what a view.

"That's right, boy, make my cock nice and wet."

He pulled it out of Tristan's mouth, running the length of his shaft down Tristan's tongue until his balls landed in his mouth, where they were eagerly sucked and slathered in saliva.

Moans of both men made my breeches uncomfortable, and I couldn't help but rearrange myself through the fabric to try to ease the discomfort.

Pulling back, Gerard paused with the head in Tristan's mouth, circling his hips, a gentle tug on the collar sliding Tristan's head a little further off the hay bale, opening his mouth wider.

"Here it comes, boy," he said as his massive length slid into Tristan's mouth. "Do you want me to stop?"

Tristan let out a desperate whine and shook his head vigorously as he clutched Gerard in his lips, his cheeks hollowing as he continued sucking on it. Gerard chuckled, "Good boy."

Tristan's throat bulged as the entire length of Gerard's shaft disappeared completely. Gerard let out a long, deep moan and dropped his head, his hair falling over Tristan's stomach. Tristan moaned around Gerard and pumped his own shaft harder. I watched hungrily as he swallowed, causing Gerard to frown and growl.

Gerard paused a moment. Just as I was becoming concerned about whether Tristan could breathe, Gerard pulled back, ropes of saliva extending between him and Tristan's mouth. Tristan gasped, his throat suddenly free of intrusion, but almost instantly, he reached his tongue up, eagerly lapping Gerard again.

"Greedy boy," Gerard chuckled as, in one smooth motion, he slid his length back down Tristan's throat. Tristan may have been the one with a cock in his mouth but, judging by Gerard's expression and the colour of his face, Tristan was in control.

Gerard's grip on the collar tightened. "Ah, Tristan, it's coming, boy." Gerard's hips popped back and forth with increased speed while Tristan's breath came out in pants and huffs.

"Come with me."

Gerard's chest muscles strained as his hips went rigid, cock still deep in Tristan's throat while Tristan's seed spilled over his stomach, his own hips twitching as he moaned out his orgasm. His throat contracted as he swallowed Gerard's release.

Huffing out the last of his orgasm, Gerard slid his shaft from Tristan, a gasp escaping Tristan as his throat cleared. Gerard leant down slowly gliding his tongue along Tristan's abs collecting the seed on his tongue, and depositing it on Tristan's lips in a passionate kiss.

Breathing heavily, Gerard stood and, moving to Tristan's side, offered him a hand in a gesture to help him up. Tristan clasped Gerard's hand and was pulled into a tight embrace.

"You did well," Gerard crooned as he removed the collar and gently kissed Tristan's nape and throat before pulling him into a tight embrace. "My sweet boy."

Heat flared in me at the familiar nickname and the passion in Gerard's voice. He stroked Tristan's hair back from his face and gazed at him.

Tristan responded by rubbing his head against Gerard's hand, eyes fixed on him, while he planted a kiss on Gerard's palm and wrapped his arms around his waist.

"What's that expression on your face? Tell me."

Tristan's cheeks coloured slightly before he quietly replied, "I enjoyed sharing this with Rook."

Gerard smiled. "So did I."

They both turned to look at me, Gerard reaching out a hand to me as Tristan rested his head against his chest. Taking Gerard's hand, I moved closer to them, admiring their handsome faces, Tristan's still flushed.

"Thank you for letting me be here with you," I whispered, glancing down at my painful erection tenting the front of my breeches and felt my face burn.

"Our desires are nothing to be ashamed of, Rook. Here we can explore them with each other, including you, if that's what you would like." Tristan reached forward to take my other hand and smiled at me. I gave them both a shy smile and nodded.

I kept thinking about Gerard's 'lesson' for days after our time in the barn. Working the fallow land proved difficult. But though the residents of the castle seemed to steal away for moments of intimacy quite often, most of the time they were deeply involved in the running of the castle. As spring progressed toward summer, Gerard and Evan came together often at the communal table to express their concerns; they oversaw castle repairs, winter preparations, and the annual check of harvest tools. One chief issue was the hay fields, and how they seemed to be suffering some strange blight.

During one such luncheon, Gerard mentioned riding out to the edge of the forest to check on the areas that were dying back. My interest was piqued.

"...if it carries on at this pace, the animals may only just have enough standing hay to last them the winter after we have taken the cut of hay we plan to store," Gerard complained.

"Hmm," Evan paused, furrowing his brow. "What concerns me is if it's having that much of an impact here, it will be worse in the outer villages. How does Harth's crops fare, Rook?"

Taken aback that they might involve me in such a serious discussion, it took me a moment to gather my thoughts. "Uh, the last couple of years have certainly seen a lower yield come harvest time. Our personal stores were nearly empty this last spring."

"I see. That's what I was afraid of," replied Evan.

"Maybe we should discuss with Mistress the need for a meeting with the elders of each of the major villages so we can lay plans for the rationing of provisions?" Gerard suggested, rubbing his hand along his jaw.

They sat for a moment, considering. I had seen the changes that Gerard spoke of, but I hadn't realised that things were so concerning that a rationing plan would be required.

"Don't look so worried, Rook. These plans may not be necessary for another couple of years yet, but it's always best to be ready, just in case." Evan patted me on the shoulder, giving it a reassuring squeeze. "This is just what it takes to assist our Mistress in taking care of the island. We worry and plan so that the others, the village folk and the younger members of our family here alike, don't have to."

"I understand," I replied. "I'm glad to be included in the conversation. I would rather know and help prepare."

A broad, proud smile spread across Evan's lips, "and that lad is one reason our Mistress favours you so. You care."

My face reddened when I noticed a similar expression of pride on Gerard's face, too. Back home, I had been scorned for what my father called 'fanciful ideals', so having my thoughts appreciated here, not only by these men who I admired but also by our Mistress, was deeply satisfying.

"Come on, lad. Mistress wants you in the meeting."

"Me! Really?" I replied, suddenly feeling sick.

"Let's not keep her waiting."

I jumped up from my seat and followed Evan and Gerard. Passing through the main hall, we entered a small chamber behind the dais. The Enchantress was seated at the head of a long table set in the middle of the room.

"Good afternoon gentlemen, take a seat."

Shaking slightly, I held back until Gerard and Evan had chosen their seats then took the one next to Gerard.

"Thank you for joining us, Rook." She gave me a small smile before turning to the others. "We need to discuss the crop issue."

"Yes, Mistress," Evan said. "Our concern is for the outer villages. If our crops are failing then who knows how those furthest from the castle are faring."

"Of course," she replied, her face full of concern. "What do you suggest?"

"I think we need to send out a request for a report from each of the major towns so we can get a clearer picture of the state of the land. I can write the announcement today and be on the road to Tride at first light."

"You do that. Thank you, Evan. And what of our own crops?"

"Mistress," Gerard cut in. "I had thought to ride out to the outer fields to assess our crop. We can decide from there whether we should cut early."

"You mean to save what we can," she replied. "At least we would have something stored. Yes, please do that Gerard."

"Of course, Mistress. I will help Evan on his way in the morning then head out myself."

"Rook, how goes the work in the West paddock?" The Enchantress asked.

"Well, Mistress. The land is now cleared. Another month to prepare the topsoil and it will be ready for planting."

"Such fast progress. What would be your suggested crop to plant?"

I was taken aback to have her ask my opinion given how relatively new the castle I was. "Given the time of year, I'd suggest an early crop of winter barley. We would have straw for the animals and the pearls for the pantry."

She beamed at me. "A sound suggestion. Thank you, Rook. Please see to it."

"Of course, Mistress."

As simple as that, she is leaving it to me.

Gods, I wish father would have been so accommodating.

"We have our plan then," she said. "Thank you all."

Allowing Gerard and Evan to rise before me, then taking my time to get up from my seat, I made my way to the Enchantress' side.

"I wanted to thank you, Mistress, for the privilege of sitting in on this council meeting. I want to do all I can to assist you."

"Your knowledge and insight are greatly appreciated here, Rook. I welcome your input."

"I was considering how we might help those who are working the land and struggling at the moment." My nerves had me talking at what felt like twice my normal speed but I was so eager to impress her. "Sometimes all that is needed is the smallest change in how the land is managed to make a huge difference."

I just couldn't seem to stop talking.

"Like the winter just gone, back in Harth, I decided to let the cows out onto the crop land during the winter days. We used less bedding, less feed, and rather than having to spread so much manure when it came time to clean out the barn in the spring, they just did some of it right there on the field making it easier for me."

Suddenly realising that I had brought up manure to the Enchantress, I grimaced and inwardly sighed and closed my eyes.

"Forgive me, Mistress," I groaned. "I hadn't intended to discuss cow manure with you."

She burst into a hearty fit of laughter that echoed around the room. Surprised and pleased that she found it so funny, and amused by the way she wiped tears from her eyes, I laughed with her.

"Oh, Rook. I do so enjoy your company," she said, wiping the last of her tears away and sharing her bright smile with me. "Thank you for sharing your ideas with me. We will wait for these reports back and then make a plan from there."

"Yes, Mistress."

"I do hope you will accept a permanent position on my council, Rook."

"It would be an honour." I bowed my head before, feeling bold, reaching forward to take her hand, grazing her knuckles with my lips.

"You may do *me* the honour of joining me in my chamber tomorrow evening," she purred.

Her change of tone registered deep within me, "I should like nothing more, Mistress."

"... take care of your saddlebags, I will ready a horse for an early departure," Gerard said as he left the kitchen.

"Much appreciated, my friend. Ah, Rook. There you are. I want you to take a rest day tomorrow, lad." Evan wrapped bread, apples and cheese in waxed cloth and packed them into the leather saddle bags laid on the table.

"You have been working hard and the West paddock looks better than it ever has thanks to your effort. The day after tomorrow, you can join Grace in the East paddock to help her with the chores but tomorrow, rest."

"Yes, Sir."

"Good lad. Hand me that waterskin will you." Using the laces sewn into the saddle bags, Evan tied the waterskin firmly in place.

"How long do you think you will be gone?" I asked.

"Oh, not long. A night, maybe two. It depends how quickly I can arrange a meeting with the elders of Tride. If I make good time I should be there well before noon tomorrow, particularly if Gerard sends me on that big mare of his. Canters as if the wind is carrying her that one." He checked the buckle holding the bedroll in place and pulled it a hole tighter.

"Might take a while for the outer villages to get back to us, but once we begin receiving replies, we can assess the situation."

I wondered how far spread people were noticing these changes. And, would they know what to do about it? If they didn't hear the announcement then it would be so much longer they would have to wait, to struggle with the difficulties the land was facing, before Evan could make contact with them.

"Hey, lad. Try not to worry, that won't help anyone. Let's see what comes of this meeting and the following reports."

I nodded, hoping the news wouldn't be too dire.

Chapter 23
Rook

The following morning we gathered in the courtyard to see Gerard and Evan off. Gerard would be back by the afternoon but Evan would be away for the night in Tride.

"So, it seems you are fitting in well around here. I hear you are a council member now," Barden said. "Should I be calling you 'Sir'?" He raised his eyebrows at me, that smile of his tugging at my own lips.

"If you like," I replied.

"Oh, I *would* like... Sir."

"Don't you have work to do or something?" I scoffed, giving his shoulder a nudge.

"Oh, and he's bossy now too," Barden replied, his pitch rising.

"Yeah, I am. Alright. So, do you have anything to do or..."

"You first."

Rolling my eyes at him, I replied, "I don't have any plans for today. Evan insisted I take the day off now that I have cleared the West paddock."

"In that case, why don't you come with me? I have something to show you."

I raised my eyebrows at him.

"Not anything like that! Although..." He paused to roll his eyes over my body a moment before straightening his face. "No, I do actually have something to show you."

I followed Barden to the weaver barn. The ground floor was full of large machines and bolts of cloth racked up along the walls. Barden led me upstairs to where he worked. He pushed a stack of clothing aside to make space on the workbench.

"Brianna arrived back yesterday and as usual she has ripped holes in every item of clothing." He rolled his eyes. "But what I wanted to show you was this."

He ferreted under the workbench and pulled out a bundle wrapped in paper. Laying it out on the table, he carefully unwrapped it and held up a deep green tunic. Its long sleeves and open neck were decorated with intricate gold embroidery and had leather laces to hold the neck closed.

"It's beautiful," I said.

"You will look very smart wearing it to the next council meeting."

"You made this... for me?"

"Mhm."

"Barden, I don't know what to... thank you. It's beautiful."

"So you said," he chuckled. "Just promise me one thing."

"What's that?"

"Don't wear it for work."

"You have my word!" I laughed.

"I have a new pair of breeches for you too and I just need to finish off the belt. If you want to stay a while I can finish it now."

He pulled towards him a gold half-moon ring which had most of a woven leather belt already attached to it. Placing a hand on the workbench beside him, I leaned closer so I could watch what he was doing.

"I just need to add a little more length to it then finish off the end."

His nimble fingers began to weave the six strands of leather together at such a pace, I could barely keep up. The belt grew longer and longer by the second.

"Your face!" Barden laughed.

"How are you doing that so fast... and without even looking?!"

"Doing it for as long as I can remember helps," he scoffed.

My own words used against me.

"Brat," I chuckled.

"Don't start that, *Sir*, or I'll never get this finished."

I stood quietly at his shoulder as he finished off the belt. He plaited the laces in such a way they ended in an elegant point before he secured the loose ends.

"There we are. Fit for a council member," he said, holding up the belt for me to see.

"Very nice. Can I try it on?" I asked, taking it from him.

"Only if you put it on over the nice new tunic and not that scruffy one you are wearing right now. I mean, did the horses chew on you or something?" He wrinkled his nose as he looked at my tunic in mock disgust.

"It will look plenty worse by the end of the season," I said, taking hold of the hem and pulling it over my head. "It will likely have more holes than Brianna's gear by the time the harvest is in."

I stood waiting a moment for him to hand me the new tunic before I realised Barden's mouth was slack, while his eyes slowly moved over my chest and abdomen.

"Nothing you haven't already seen," I chuckled, clicking my fingers in front of his face to get his attention.

"Mmm... couldn't appreciate the view properly when you were down in the paddock though," he replied, slowly handing me the new tunic.

"Tss, give that here," I replied, taking the tunic from him and pulling it on to hide my rising blush.

The new linen was stiff but soft and lay nicely against my skin.

"That looks to fit rather well. And with the belt, the length should be perfect." Barden said, handing me the newly finished belt. I wrapped it around my waist before securing it at the front.

"You do my work justice," Barden said with a flourish, making me laugh. He smiled before adding, in a more serious tone, "You look very handsome, Rook. Truly."

"Thank you... Barden. For the tunic and..."

His eyes had glazed over as I stared down at him. I watched them slide from my lips to my eyes and back again repeatedly. There was something about him that was so very inviting. I felt an ease in his company and a strong pull to be close to him. Leaning forward, I pressed my lips lightly to his, their warmth melting against mine. His lips were as soft as I expected them to be and his smell was light and sweet like fresh mint leaves.

"Rook," he murmured against my lips.

Drawing back, I ran my hand over his cheek. His skin was smooth against my hand, which was no doubt rough with callouses to his soft skin but he didn't seem to mind.

"Mmm, such strong, warm hands," he whispered.

I took in the details of his face from this close, the marble of blues that swirled through his eyes, a small, faint scar across his cheek, and a light dusting of day-old stubble over his sharp jaw.

"Kiss me again. Please." Barden whined.

Glowing with triumph and desire, I leaned down again to kiss him. Spurred on, he stood, wrapping his arms around my neck and pushing his lips more forcefully to mine, coaxing them open to slide his tongue over mine. Groaning and welcoming his embrace, I gripped his waist to hold him to me.

Gods, he feels good.

His firm chest pressed to mine, his needy lips and his small moans sent tendrils of heat right through me which threatened to push me over the edge. Pulling back, overwhelmed and needing to catch my breath, I rested my forehead against his to steady myself.

This man. He stirs things in me that I didn't know were there.

His eyes full of lust, Barden smiled, a sweet but loving smile with just a small hint of his mischief, "You taste like sweet apples."

Gerard returned to the barn late afternoon but was still keen to see me begin my training with the young horses.

"Right, boy, the four new youngsters are on their own in there. I have shut the rest of the horses in the corral so they won't come and steal all the treats from you," Gerard explained as he handed me a bucket of fruit scraps. "Take this and sit in the middle over there with something tasty in your hand and wait to see if one of them comes over to you."

"So, just sit there and feed them treats," I replied.

"Yup. We just want them to associate people with something good, and those apple cores are nice and sweet."

Nodding, I ducked under the fence into the section of the barn where the four young horses were. Their ears pricked, and their eyes followed me as I slowly made my way to the middle and settled myself in the straw with the bucket of scraps. Satisfied I wasn't coming their way, they continued nosing around the straw, picking up the odd strand.

They were quite a variety of colours. The one closest to me had a sleek black coat and a long mane that fell over his eyes. Hiding behind him were four bright chestnut legs and the tips of two ears that kept flicking in my direction. A stride behind the chestnut, a nearly completely white pony, save for a big brown patch over one of his eyes, was having his butt used as a scratching post by a little grey pony who was vigorously rubbing her head against him. The dapples over her flank looked like a sheet of paper that had been left out in the rain, smudged circular droplets seeped into the hair surrounding them as though they were running ink.

Smiling and breathing in their dusty smell, I rummaged around in the bucket for an apple core, selecting a particularly big one hoping to entice one of them over. Glancing for a moment over to Gerard, who was grooming one of the horses at the other end of the barn, my attention was pulled back by a rustling beside me. Ahead of the others, one youngster was steadily creeping towards me, looking right at me, ears pricked. Aside from the white snip on his nose, he was black as the forest at night. Strands of mane hung over his large, curious eyes, and he puffed through his nose, taking in my smell. Each step he took was tentative, and not wanting to intimidate him with my eager gaze, I cast my eyes away from him.

The rustling continued intermittently for a few minutes before I couldn't help but steal another glance towards him. The youngster had stopped a few feet from me, barely moving, its nostrils twitching continuously as he took in my smell and, no doubt, the smell of the apple core in my hand.

Carefully sliding my hand out, I opened my palm to reveal the core and waited. Silence for a moment made me question whether the youngster would feel comfortable enough to approach me, despite the lure of the sweet treat. But all too soon I heard the familiar rustling of the straw, then hot breath on my outstretched hand followed by lips gently taking the core.

Happiness welled in me, and a wide smile spread across my face. I noticed Gerard watching and silently cheering and giving me a thumbs up. Not wanting to giggle and scare the youngster, I turned my attention back to the bucket to quietly select another core and eased my hand out in the pony's direction, hoping my movements wouldn't frighten him and make him back away. Warm breath on my hand, followed by satisfied munching, filled me with pride.

The black youngster took three more cores from me in this manner before he was brave enough to come closer. His nose travelled up my arm, breathing in deep puffs as he took in more of my smell before nosing my hair. He paused, gently nudging my head with his lip while I held stock still not wanting to discourage him.

The other horses were happy in their task of combing through the straw while, as the minutes ticked by, this young colt stood with me, nose in my hair. Little by little, his nose dipped lower until it finally rested on my shoulder. As he relaxed, his nose became heavier against me, and feeling confident my movement wouldn't disturb him, I slowly turned my face towards him.

The soft skin and fine hair of his muzzle were warm against my cheek. Resting my nose against his, we shared our breath the way I had seen Gerard do with Bandaa. I could have burst with delight that this youngster wanted to share this gentle interaction with me. Closing my eyes, I sat peacefully with my companion, honoured by his trust in me.

One of the other horses, no doubt smelling the sweet treats I had in the bucket, ventured a little closer to us, disturbing our quiet moment. Not wanting the others to miss out, I cast a couple of cores into the straw a few feet from me for the others to find. Knowing they were unlikely to come closer to look for them while I was still there, I eased myself to standing and steadily made my way towards the fence, glancing back to see the black colt watching my departure, ears and eyes trained on me.

As I reached the fence, Gerard didn't make a move to join me and had a look of anticipation on his face as I approached. Only when I stopped did I realise something else was rustling the straw. Glancing over my shoulder, a familiar snip of white on an otherwise black nose was reaching up to my shoulder to sniff my hair. Delighted, I didn't move and was rewarded with a velvety nose nuzzling its way along the back of my neck before he quietly wandered back to the others.

"I think that one likes you, boy. Why don't you pick out a name for him?"

"Really?"

"Sure, I think it's clear he has chosen you as his human."

I hadn't named a horse before. The horse we had back home was older than me and I just referred to him as 'old man'. "What did you call your first youngster?" I asked.

"Ah, my first youngster was a fabulous horse. His name was Siedon, and he was the first youngster I took on when I started buying horses in for breeding. He was gangly and unruly but his conformation was spot on and boy did he mature into something special. He was Bandaa's father. He passed a couple of years ago, found him out in the pasture surrounded by the herd just laying quietly. It felt like the end. Sat myself down at his side and stayed with him while he passed. I think he had been waiting for me."

"Would you mind if I named this little guy after him?" I asked.

"It would be a pleasure to call his name across the paddock again," Gerard beamed. "You got yourself a good one there. He is the strongest and most curious of all the youngsters. You keep coming out here and spending time with him, he will be coming to your call in no time."

"I can keep working with him?"

"If you want to. I can help you, point you in the right direction as you need it. Trust is the first thing you need in any relationship. Keep working on that for a while and see how you get on."

"I will. Thanks, Gerard."

"You're welcome. Now, let's leave these guys to eat and grab some food ourselves."

Chapter 25

Rook

"**G**ood evening, Rook." My Mistress' voice raised goosebumps over my naked skin as I stood before her.

"Good evening, Mistress." My words came out in a whisper. It had been a long day anticipating this meeting with her.

She was seated on the sofa in front of the fire in her chamber, legs crossed, with her toes resting on the edge of the table in front of her, her slip dress riding high, exposing her thighs. Behind her were the two nymph-like forms of Grace and Brianna. Their smiles filled with heat and I fixed my eyes once again upon her, trying hard to remain composed under the gaze of these three beautiful women.

"It seems you enjoyed your time in the barn with Gerard and Tristan."

My face flushed, and I fumbled with my fingers clenched behind my back.

How did she know that?

"Yes, Mistress."

"I enjoyed it too," she purred.

She was there?

"Since you enjoyed it so much, I have thought of something else you might enjoy and have asked Grace and Brianna to join us."

Has she been watching me?

The thought of my Mistress following me and watching me while I enjoyed the company of the others had my cock bobbing in response. Grace and Brianna giggled quietly. Their eyes roamed my thighs, causing my face to burn all the more.

"Yes, yes, girls. You can play with him in a moment," she chuckled to them, momentarily glancing in their direction before setting her emerald eyes on me again. "Tonight, my darling Rook, it would be my pleasure to bind you to this table."

She gestured to the table in front of her, running the tips of her fingers along the smooth wooden surface and over a metal ring fixed in one of the corners, before pulling from behind her a pair of black leather cuffs. Each cuff had a ring attached to one side and a buckle on the other. My jaw went slack in surprise as my eyes flicked between her eager face and the cuffs in her hand.

Well, this is new.

Aside from the restriction from another's body pushed against mine, I hadn't been restrained before. Being bound to a table at the mercy of these three women wasn't what had sprung to mind as I had waited to hear my Mistress speak, but imagining what it might entail excited me. Licking my lips, I nodded.

Leaning forward and slowly curling her index finger, she gestured for me to come to her. Nervous, breath shallow, and hot with anticipation,

I stepped forward to stand directly in front of her, all too aware of my growing erection that was reaching out to her. Grazing her eyes over my cock before fixing them on mine, she held open each cuff in turn for me to slide my arm into before buckling them snuggly around my wrists. Once they were in place, I turned my wrists over, inspecting the padded leather.

These look as well crafted as Gerard's collar. I wonder if he made these too?

Shaken out of my thoughts by Grace and Brianna giggling again, I looked back to my Mistress, a shy smile spreading across my lips at having lost myself for a moment.

"Comfortable, aren't they? My horse master is a skilled craftsman."

"He is." Hesitating a moment, I continued. "He has offered for me to learn from him when he makes his next piece."

"Has he indeed?" her smile broadened. "Well, we will have to commission him to make something extra special then, won't we?" her hooded eyes darkened.

Grace and Brianna glanced at each other, knowing grins passing between them.

The Enchantress took a cushion from the sofa and placed it at one end of the table. "Rest your head here, please, my darling," she patted the cushion, summoning me.

Moving to obey, I sat at the end of the table, lay my back down against the smooth and surprisingly warm wood and rested my head on the cushion.

"Raise your hands above your head, my love."

Looking up to where the rings were fixed in each corner of the table just above my head, I reached my hands up to rest each cuff on a ring. My excitement was mixed with slight concern as I lay in this prone position, imagining what it would be like once my arms were fixed and I couldn't move.

"I am going to fix your cuffs to these rings in a moment, but before I do, I want you to show me the hand signal that Tristan demonstrated to Gerard as the signal to stop," said the Enchantress, a serious tone in her voice.

Relief washed over me and with my hands still resting above my head, I showed her the vee signal with my index and middle finger. She smiled.

"You may be restrained, but you can stop what is happening at any moment if it becomes too much, ok?"

Nodding, I replied, "Yes, Mistress."

"Good boy."

The sound of clunking metal signalled my restriction, and as she moved to my other hand, I experimentally tested the hand that was already fixed. The leather cuff didn't shift as I pulled against it, and the padding was comfortable. My other hand fixed into position, the Enchantress moved to kneel on the floor at the end of the table near my head. I gazed at her as she ran her hand over my cheek before kissing my lips.

"I am looking forward to watching you squirm," she purred, turning my head towards Grace and Brianna while she rested her cheek on my temple. "Now, my sweet girls are going to be allowed to play with that pretty cock of yours, but... we are going to make a game out of how long it will take for you to release your seed." A groan escaped my lips, and turning my head back to look at her, she crooned, "I can see how tight your balls are, darling, but it would please me to see you squirm and hear you moan. You do want to please me, don't you, Rook?"

"Yes, Mistress." I was all too aware of the whine in my voice at my admission, but my desire had been pent up since witnessing Gerard and Tristan's intimate coupling in the barn, and I was eager for release.

"Good boy. Girls, his cock is yours until I require his seed."

Grace and Brianna sprang from behind the sofa, shedding their clothes as they came towards me, and knelt on the floor on either side of my hips, a hungry look on their faces.

Shit.

Intimidated but aroused, I looked between them while they paused, their delicate faces alive with mischief before they pounced. Brianna sank her teeth into my thigh while Grace slid her lips to the root of my cock, taking all of me in her mouth.

I growled as the sharp ache in my thigh shot through my leg but was interrupted by the sudden and fast pace of Grace's mouth slipping up and down my rigid shaft. My hips bucked up against them, which dislodged the girls from me for a moment. Laughing, they wrapped their hands around my thighs, pushed me back down and continued their torment.

Gritting my teeth, I tried to relax into the sensations. As I became used to the pain in my thigh, the tingle through my cock increased. I swelled in Grace's mouth, and as Brianna's delicate fingers wrapped around my balls, I couldn't hold back a moan. As the moan escaped my lips, the girls released me and sat back. Perplexed, I looked down to see them sitting still, watching me.

After another moment's pause and a glance at each other, they grabbed me again. Brianna sunk her teeth into the softer flesh of my inner thigh as Grace rolled her tongue around my cock, soaking it in her saliva. Sucking in a breath, I tried to stay still and ride the sensation, but I couldn't help the tension in my legs as I strained against the table, raising my hips towards Grace.

Giggling, they sat back again, and in an exacerbated gasp I released the breath I had been holding. Panting, I looked between them and then up to my Mistress.

"Do you want them to stop, Rook?"

I shook my head.

"I want to hear you say it."

"I don't want them to stop," I replied in a quiet but urgent voice.

Instantly, the girls were on me again. This time, they both wrapped their lips around my cock, tilting their heads to the side so they could kiss each other with me between their lips. Their tongues wound around the underside of my shaft, their lips straining around me as they tried to touch each other, their tongues lapping at me. Their delicate hands slid up my chest as their mouths set a rhythm up and down in tandem. Warm hands slid down my cheeks and under my chin, putting pressure there to tilt my head back. Panting, I gazed into my Mistress' eyes, full of their usual heat.

As my pleasure mounted and I started to leak, small fingers squeezed hard on my nipples, making me jump and hiss. All touch went away instantly, once again pulling a groan from me. Eager for release, I fruitlessly raised my hips and groaned again. The girl's reply was only to smirk.

Feeling a little desperate, I gave my Mistress an imploring look. Grinding my hips against the air and holding her gaze, I groaned again, my voice cracking, "Mistress... please..."

Her voice heavy and her eyes hooded, she purred, "You look so pretty when you beg, darling." Biting her lip, she smiled. "Turn over and kneel on the table."

Eager as ever to obey her, I shimmied my body awkwardly sideways so I could roll onto my tummy, my arms now folded as they were still shackled to the corners of the table, and slid my knees under myself. Elbows resting on the table, knees under my hips, I settled with my chin down onto my forearms, ass in the air, feeling exposed but desperate for my Mistress to touch me.

She stood and moved along my side, sliding her hand over my back and squeezing my ass as she knelt beside my hip. Her fingers kneaded my flesh, moving from one cheek to the other before sliding her hand between my legs to grasp my balls, making me jump. Straining my hips backwards, I tried to increase the amount of pressure with which she was touching me, but her touches were maddeningly soft. The movement of her hand mimicked the movement I remember watching the milkmaid do to the milking cows. This thought made me blush.

"So firm...so full of seed for me."

"Yes, Mistress." I croaked, eager for her to continue.

Wrapping her hand around the wet head of my shaft, she rolled it around the swollen end, coating me in my own juices before sliding her hand to the base of my cock and back again, continuing her milking of my balls.

Fuck, this feels so good. I won't last long.

"Remind me of the signal you should use if you want everything to stop, Rook."

Sliding my hand over so she could see it from where she sat, I made the vee signal with my fore and middle finger.

"Good boy. Do you want me to stop?" she purred, continuing her all too steady pace, teasing me.

Quickly clenching my fingers into a fist, I hissed, "No, Mistress!"

At my words, the pace of her hand pumping my shaft increased. I had to make a conscious effort not to grind my hips against her in my needy attempt to reach my satisfaction sooner. As the embers of my climax began to build, hands slid up the backs of my thighs and massaged my cheeks, making me start. I had forgotten about Grace and Brianna!

Their small fingers dancing across my skin added tingles of pleasure to the already growing sensation through my hips and thighs. Groaning my appreciation, I rested my forehead down against my arms, relaxing into their touches. Touches that became wet when they replaced their fingers with their tongues, making me draw a sharp breath. In their lapping motion, Grace and Brianna's tongues travelled steadily inward and, coupled with my Mistress' continued attention, pushed my climax closer.

This is... unexpected... and surprisingly... so fucking good.

Their teasing tongues edged closer together, moving over steadily more sensitive skin. Increasing the pace of their lapping, they moved closer still until their tongues met, warm and wet, rolling around each other over my entrance.

"Fuuuuck," I growled.

I didn't know girls did this.

Barely able to contain myself, I was vaguely aware I was gritting my teeth and straining against the cuffs as I pulled back against them, trying to increase the pressure of their touches. My breath came out in gasps as my passion reached its peak.

"Mistress! I... I can't... I'm going to..."

As swiftly as the words came out of my mouth, she removed her hand and wrapped her mouth around me instead. Pleasure exploded through me as I pumped my cock deeper into my Mistress' mouth, filling her throat with my seed.

Arching my back, I looked down to see her beautiful face, eyes on me, suckling on my shaft, a small trail of shining fluid leaking from the corner of her mouth.

Grunting out the last of my ejaculation, I watched as she slid away from me, licking her lips as she stood up and moved round to the head of the table again. Lips still shining, she leant forward and opened her mouth to show me the seed I had deposited there before sliding her tongue over my open lips, covering them in my own seed.

Her voice came thick and heavy with desire. "When you feel your lips tingling tomorrow, you will think of this moment where we both have your seed in our mouths."

A tremor of pleasure shook my body, and my cock bobbed wildly in response to her, "Yes, Mistress."

Chapter 26
Enchantress

D elicious.

If only it could last.

It tastes so sweet but dissipates so quickly.

If only it was enough.

The land suffers and I feel powerless to help. What little of myself I have to give isn't enough. It's never enough.

Chapter 27
Rook

"**P**roduce fit for the horn of plenty," Grace proclaimed as she gestured out across the field with a sweep of her hand the following morning.

We stood in the East paddock, a smaller, more managed field. Instead of unmanaged scrub, this field was full of neat rows of crops, many of which I could identify from where I was standing on the raised stone steps. The castle walls surrounded this field as they did the meadow and the East paddock. Grace looked at me expectantly, waiting for a response.

"It's very well organised and is growing well," I replied, smiling down at her.

She beamed with a thrilled look on her face. "Thanks, I love being out here. The Mistress' magic makes the plants grow, but I keep the paths clear, prune the beds and pick things as they mature. It's a lot of work to keep it tidy, but a couple of the others help me from time to time when they are done with their own chores. But it will be a tremendous help to have someone here all the time. The hardest times are planting and harvesting, but I guess you already knew that!"

"Sure do." I grinned back at her. Her excitement was an endearing trait. I was pleased to see how much she loved being out here. Most of my fondest memories came from being out on the land, even though farming was hard work and there was always something to do. It was refreshing to meet a girl like Grace, who wasn't only not afraid of the hard work that comes with farming, but also seemed to enjoy it, too. Most of the girls back home grumbled about fieldwork, making excuses why they weren't working or flirting with the men to have them do their chores for them. I had never been a hard master to those who had worked for me, and I didn't demand they stay if they didn't want to, but it was always hard work when the women folk insisted they needed the pay but then didn't do the work.

"Right, can you please fill this basket with strawberries from the trellis and I'll get the things Evan needs for supper."

The trellis made up a long, screened tunnel that was shaded by a canopy full of rich green leaves dotted with a mixture of white flowers, green buds and bright red strawberries. With the tips of my fingers, I gently brushed the delicate flowers and tiny green strawberries, their texture bumpy under the pad of my fingers. Picking an enormous, bright red strawberry, I took a bite, licking the juice that dribbled down my chin. I closed my eyes, slowly crushing it with my tongue against the roof of my mouth, savouring the juice as it trickled down my throat.

"I could watch you do that all day," came the voice of the Enchantress from beside me.

I spun around and choked on the juice I was still swallowing.

"Sorry, my darling," she said, stepping towards me, a slight chuckle in her voice, "I didn't mean to make you jump."

"I'm fine," I sputtered, "I'm alright," smiling at her when I saw she was grinning.

Her thin dress clung to her slender body. My greedy eyes roamed over her form as I wiped the remaining juice from my chin.

She stepped closer to me, placing a hand on my chest and looking up into my eyes. My breath went shallow, and my body tensed at having her so close to me. Keeping her eyes on mine, she inclined her chin towards my hand, still holding half the strawberry, and opened her mouth. I swallowed hard and slowly brought the strawberry to her mouth, watching as her lips closed around it and sucked on it gently.

She took her time sucking the rest of the strawberry from its stalk and licked her lips. My mind flashed with images of the previous evening. Without thought, I grabbed her throat just below her jaw and slowly pushed to lift her chin towards me. The Enchantress drew a sudden breath. With desire burning through me, I leaned forward and ran my tongue over her lips in long slow strokes, tasting the sweet juice on her plump lips. She let out a long sigh and took hold of my hips, pulling me close to her.

My chest heaved as my passion boiled. My hand squeezed her throat just a little firmer as I bit down on her lip, a growl escaping from my chest. She gasped and pulled back from me. My mind suddenly returned, and I realised what I had done.

"Oh shit, I'm so sorry," I stammered, blinking rapidly, "I couldn't help it, I...I..."

Fuck! What the fuck did you just do?!

Fear coursed through me, and words failed me.

You fucking BIT her!

Why would you do that?!

Holding my breath, I waited for her response, hoping the reprimand wouldn't be too severe. The Enchantress's eyes darkened with what seemed to be passion rather than anger. "There's no need to apologise, my sweet," she purred, smiling and rubbing her tongue along her lip where I had bitten her. "I'm sure I will think of a way for you to make it up to me."

I smiled sheepishly, scrubbing my hand through my hair, relieved that I hadn't overstepped but also excited by her response. "Yes, Mistress," I replied, my heart hammering in my chest.

"Hmm," she crooned at me. "Let me help you fill your basket."

She turned away from me and began plucking the ripe fruit from overhead while I reached to do the same, not taking my eyes off her. Her delicate fingers gently wrapped around each fruit, expertly twisted and pulled the strawberry from its stalk, holding it tenderly in her hand as she reached for the next. Seeming to sense I was staring at her, she looked over at me and smiled.

Gods, she is beautiful.

Just as she had commanded me to the evening before, I couldn't help but remember my seed coating both our lips.

When she turned away, I noticed a somewhat sad look on her face.

"Are you well, Mistress?"

She spun back to me and replied, "Yes," but hesitated for a moment, mouth slightly open as if there was more she was considering saying.

Suddenly she looked small to me, almost childlike, a sadness in her eyes. Stepping forward, closing the gap between us, I gently wrapped my arms around her shoulders and held her tight. She sighed and leaned into me, causing my chest to swell.

"I would do anything to make your burden easier to bear," I whispered, squeezing her a little tighter.

She pulled back to look into my eyes sweeping a lock of my hair off my forehead "Oh, my darling," she said. "Those tender eyes see so much."

She ran her hand down my cheek and leaned in to kiss me, sucking my lip into her mouth and sliding her tongue around mine. Spurred on, I wrapped my arms tighter around her and leaned into her. Her taste, mixed with the strawberry, made a sweet flavour in my mouth. I put my hand in her hair, forcing her forwards so I could crush my mouth harder to hers. Then she bit down hard.

"Hmph," I groaned, pulling away and tasting blood.

The corner of her mouth tilted up as she stared at me from under her lashes with a look that reminded me she was still Mistress here.

"Come to my chamber tomorrow evening, precious. I want to taste more of that beautiful body."

I grinned. "Yes, Mistress."

"Good boy," she whispered and walked away.

I stared after her, my thighs tingling and my now rock-hard cock bulging against my breeches. Watching her go up the steps and into the courtyard, I was filled with a sudden impulsive urge and glancing around to see Grace busy at the other end of the paddock, I went after her.

Reaching the top of the steps, I saw her going through the archway that led out into the forest. Jogging down the steps as swiftly and quietly as possible, I stopped just before the archway and peered around the edge.

I didn't know what possessed me to follow her and I was concerned what she would say if she saw me, but my body burned with a heat that didn't want to be parted from her. I also wanted to know more about her, the true her and following her seemed like a good way to find out. She disappeared into the trees and, taking off my shoes to soften my steps, I ran after her.

The path wound its way through the trees, ducking around the patches of sunlight and stopping periodically, I soon caught up with her unseen. Seeing her standing still on the path, I paused behind a bush, peering through the leaves to see her. She stood with her head turned slightly to the side as if listening. I held my breath.

Her lips curved slightly in a small smile before she turned and carried on. Waiting until she was a little way along and about to go out of sight, I came from my hiding place and headed towards a wide tree on the opposite side of the path as she disappeared around it. Stopping when I reached it, I slowly tilted my head around the tree.

She had paused again, just before a fork in the path, head turned as if listening again. A brief look over her shoulder and what looked like a devious grin on her face gave me the distinct impression that I maybe wasn't being as subtle as I thought.

Shit, she knows.

Before my worry could engulf me, she turned fully around for a moment, giggled and then ran down the left-hand path.

Is she playing with you?

Oh, hell yes!

Excitement flooded me, and I charged after her. Rounding the corner, I saw her running form disappearing behind a huge blackberry thicket, her laughter ringing out through the forest.

Gods, this woman!

The sheer delight of running through this beautiful forest after the Enchantress whose magic makes it bloom while she giggled at the thought of being followed by me had laughter of pure joy escape me, echoing with hers around us.

I flew around the curve in the path, only to find I could no longer see her. Frowning, I jerked my head around, trying to find her. A few moments of silence passed before I heard a whistle coming from a path hidden behind some bushes.

Is she whistling at you... like a... dog?

Fuck, why did that make my cock so hard?!

Gently pushing through the bushes, I stalked along the new path, eyes scanning the forest for her. The trail didn't go far until it reached a small clearing where the river cut through the trees and made a pool. The Enchantress had stopped at the edge of the water, her head tilted back, her eyes closed. I stepped off the path into a bush and crouched down, finding a spot where I could look through the leaves and watch her.

She stood, face turned up towards the sunlight reaching through the trees before she slid her hands under the straps of her dress and allowed it to fall to the ground. My breath caught in my throat, and my heart pounded at the sight of her. Her skin shone in the sunlight as though her body were metallic, the light glinting off her.

She glanced back, a serene look on her face, before striding out into the river, gliding the tips of her fingers along the surface as she went deeper into the water. Stopping before she was out of her depth, she laid her head back, wetting her hair. I could see the mound of her breasts beyond her face and watched as the water lapped around them, giving me fleeting glances of her nipples. Barely breathing, I stared at this beautiful creature before me. She was perfection.

After a minute of laying on the surface of the water, she slowly lifted her head and stood up, her body and hair glistening with droplets of water that shone like gemstones. She turned slightly so I could see her face, her head bowed, and her eyes closed. There I saw the same sadness in her face again that I had seen back at the castle. It was silent around us as if the entire forest was waiting for something. She took a deep breath, and to my surprise, she sang. A long, mournful sound filled my eyes with tears and my soul with loneliness as her voice began low. It pierced my heart with a sorrowful tale of solitude and desire, its mixture of low tones blending gently into one another, creating a continuous sound. Her breasts heaved as she took a deep breath and increased her pitch and volume. Her voice carried around the trees and seemed to reverberate off them, surrounding me. It penetrated me, reached into my body and made my muscles tremble and my breath rattle, and filled me with sadness and longing.

There was a moment's pause in which the Enchantress took another deep breath, slowly tilted her face upwards towards the sun, and a smile spread across it, and her voice changed. A lighter, higher pitch echoed through the clearing making my heart swell and pound harder in my chest. Her voice, now full of happiness and pleasure, was warm and hopeful. The sound seemed to go on forever, and I closed my eyes in an attempt to hold on to the notes and hear them more clearly.

It was a few moments before I realised I was sitting in silence. Slowly, the sound of the river and the wind blowing lazily through the trees came back to me, and I opened my eyes. The Enchantress was gone. I looked around quickly, trying to see her, but couldn't. Standing up, I looked in every direction and made my way down to the river. She was gone, and I was alone, but standing where she had stood, with the sun warming me and her voice still swirling around in my head, I smiled. There was hope.

Chapter 28

Rook

Back in the kitchen, I found Gerard and Evan deep in conversation while setting out food along the tables.

"...able to meet with them right away. After giving me an hour of their time I retired early and was able to set off before sunrise this morning. They began work on the letters right away and assured me they would go out the next day," Evan explained.

"Did they show concern over the matter?" Gerard replied, a frown furrowing his brow.

"Mildly, they said there had been a small increase in the price of produce from the local farmers come market day but nothing significant enough to be concerning."

"I'll be interested to see what other folk further afield have to say. Hey, Rook. Are you ok, boy? You look pale," Gerard asked.

"I...uhm...I followed Mistress down to the river," I admitted in a daze, feeling myself blush, embarrassed but knowing I should admit it.

Gerard's face softened. "She is a beauty beyond all others. No one who comes into her service can help but fall in love with her," he said gently, with understanding in his voice.

"She sang," I said, a hollow feeling in my chest at the inability to do her voice justice.

"Ah," said Evan. "Yes, that is something only a few of us have had the pleasure to witness, however conflicting an experience it is."

"Mmm, indeed," said Gerard, "We do our best to love our Mistress, but we cannot make up for the absence of her mate."

I frowned, "Her mate?"

"Yes, her true mate. The Alpha that seeks to claim her."

Confused, I eagerly pressed him, "What do you mean by her true mate?"

"Well, the thing is, lad, in living memory, our Mistress has never been known to take a mate. I have been here for many years, faithfully serving her, and I have never known her to be intimate with anyone. She kisses and caresses, but no more. Her pleasure comes from our pleasure. She watches us, instructs us and spurs us on but doesn't take part in the acts herself. All of us here long to be the one to please her with such intimacy, but she does not wish it. It pains me to see loneliness in our Mistress' heart."

I couldn't take in what I was hearing, "I don't understand."

She has never taken a lover?

Is this why she has such sadness hidden in her eyes?

Is she lonely?

"What Evan says is true. Our Mistress, as far as I am aware, has never taken a mate. She relishes our pleasure and orchestrates us as she pleases to fuel her magic but does not partake. It is part of our service here that we care for and give ourselves to her, but she takes no more than fleeting touches and kisses for herself. She tells me that when the one she waits for comes, she will know it."

Gerard and Evan's words turned over in my mind. I just couldn't imagine the Enchantress never taking a lover. She was a true beauty; she must have had no end of people that would want to take care of her and love her, she surely had her pick of whoever she wanted.

Well, sure, she has people who care for and love her, but she hasn't met the one person she wants to be intimate with. The one soul who connects with hers. The one that sparks the light inside her.

This all sounds rather familiar.

Jealousy suddenly burned through me as I recalled Gerard's words.

Who was the unworthy fuck that would come to try to claim her as his?! Her Alpha? The warrior who should have been here but instead has neglected his duty to protect her.

She was magnificent, beyond all others. No one compared to her, the Enchantress, our silver-haired goddess, my Mistress. No one would ever be good enough for her.

I needed to work. I needed to do something to clear my mind. Grace stayed in the kitchen to have breakfast, but I couldn't eat. My stomach clenched, my mind a blur; I needed to be outside.

We had planned on turning over the bed at the far end of the paddock. It was going to be hard work, and knowing the physical effort would distract me, that was my plan. I found the hoe and went to work. Swinging it high above my head. Feeling the blade sink deep into the earth was very satisfying. The sharp blade cut through the limp plants and sliced through the dark topsoil, ripping it open as I pulled the blade back out. As I moved along the bed, the heavy soil became churned up and mixed in with the old plants, giving out a rich smell that filled my nostrils, flared from the effort.

As the sun climbed higher, the sweat dripped down my back. This was relaxing to me, this well-known feeling that felt like home. My hands, calloused from years on the farm, felt no pain as I swung the hoe with a satisfying feeling of exertion. This I could do. If there was nothing else that I could contribute, this I could do.

I continued moving through the bed, breaking up the clumps of earth as I turned over the topsoil. My shoulders and arms warmed as my muscles worked. A slight ache was building in my shoulder blades as I neared the castle wall. I challenged myself to make it to the wall before resting in the shade it provided.

The repetition of the work and the effort needed to cut through the soil did the job of clearing my mind perfectly. I watched the blade of the hoe disappear and, with satisfaction, felt the soil glide open and break down, neatly turning the earth.

When at last I reached the patch of shade near the wall, my shoulders were glowing and my back was wet with sweat. My mind eased, I was ready for a rest. Dropping the hoe, I slumped against the wall, the coolness of the stone refreshing against my skin.

I looked up at the same clear sky I would look upon back home out in the fields. This place was out of a dream, but no amount of dreaming could have prepared me for the Enchantress. She loved so deeply, felt so deeply, yet kept so much hidden. Not unlike me. I had spent years back home wishing to meet someone I could connect with, someone who loved the natural world as much as I did and found comfort and happiness surrounded by it. I wanted to share this feeling with someone, and I harboured a hope that it would be her, here, in this beautiful place.

That hope was tinged with a bitter aftertaste though.

But I can't take away her sadness.

How I wish I could.

Movement in the corner of my eye made me jump, pulling me out of my thoughts. Barden came closer.

"Did I scare you, handsome?" He winked and handed me a waterskin. The ice-cold water was just what I needed. I thanked him for his thoughtfulness.

"No need to thank me, honey. I'm glad of the chance to have some alone time with you," he said as he shuffled close enough to brush his thigh against mine.

I held his gaze a moment, delighted by the contact.

"So, what's on your mind?"

"Who said I had anything on my mind?" I replied, looking away.

"The soil you just tore apart. And that frown on your face."

I groaned. "It's just... I want to help Mistress but... what if it's not enough?" I didn't want to say, 'What if I'm not enough?' and sound morose, but from the look Barden gave me I may as well have.

"Mistress accepted you into service here, invited you to be a member of the council, has put you in charge of our agriculture, can't keep her eyes off you and insists on your offerings... *regularly,*" Barden said, checking off his fingers as he went. "Tell me again why you're not enough?"

"Alright, alright," I laughed. "Enough!"

"Good," he replied, giving his head a firm nod in my direction, just to drive his point home.

He was right of course. Mistress was happy with my service to her, she had told me as much, so all I could do was hope my efforts continued to be helpful to her.

I also held hopes beyond my Mistress. She was the sun that we all revolved around but, as I stole glances at Barden, I felt a longing that had me imagining a future that involved him. He caught my eye and I couldn't stop my grin as I looked away, trying to hide it.

"You really are so handsome when you smile like that, Rook," he said, his voice soft. "It just makes me want to kiss every inch of your face."

"Then why don't you," I muttered, eager for his touch.

He adjusted his hips so he could lean towards me and brought his lips close enough to mine that I could feel his breath. He stayed there a moment, sultry eyes locked onto mine, then turning his head, moving his lips to my ear. My breath was shallow, and my chest tight as I relished his closeness.

"She's watching," he breathed quietly against my ear, gently brushing his lips along my cheek as he sat back.

"Who?" I asked.

"You know who," Barden replied, looking at me through his lashes. "You know how our Mistress enjoys... watching."

She's watching.

"I have been thinking about you," Barden murmured, "And I think you have been thinking about me."

I couldn't deny that. I had thought of him, often. He was an attractive man, lithe and graceful. Since our first kiss, I had wanted to hold him again.

"I have also seen how you keep looking at me." His voice even softer, a breathy whisper that stroked my face as his sweet smell made me salivate.

"And I'll bet..." he replied. "If I offered to suck that perfect prick of yours... you wouldn't say no."

Fuck.

Barden placed his hand gently on my thigh and I couldn't hold back. I grabbed him, pushing my lips hard to his, my hand on the back of his neck, holding him tight to me. He kissed me back, his soft lips moulding around mine as his hand slid up my leg and rubbed at me through the fabric of my breeches.

"Take it out," I growled as I got to my feet, keeping my lips on his for as long as possible before standing.

I towered over him, his smouldering gaze holding mine as he curled his fingers under my waistband, grazing my abs before tugging my breeches down slowly. The tip of my cock remained trapped as he pulled them down, my hair and the base of my shaft exposed first. The air against my flesh raised goosebumps across my skin.

Barden leant forward, placing a gentle kiss on the exposed part of my cock, eyes fixed on mine, before pulling my breeches down just enough to free me. I moaned at the soft, barely there touch.

"Ever the tease," I muttered through clenched teeth.

He admired me before slowly opening his mouth and sticking out his tongue. He paused, looking me in the eye, mouth wide... then winked.

A prickle of heat ran through my stomach in response. I spread my feet to steady myself before closing the gap between my swollen head and the tip of his tongue.

His tongue was wide and wet. It hugged the underside of my shaft as I slid easily past his lips. I paused, groaning as he closed his lips around me and swallowed, squeezing my cock with his entire mouth. He took hold of my hips and slowly moved his head towards me, taking more of me in his mouth. At any moment, I expected him to stop, but I felt the tip of my cock hit the roof of his mouth and keep going. He pushed it further until it slid down his throat, my full length inside him. I slammed my hand against the wall to steady myself as he swallowed, his throat constricting around me, sending sharp ripples of sensation pulsing through my thighs and abdomen.

"Fuuuuck, Barden," I growled.

Gritting my teeth, I sucked in a breath as he hummed, sending fiery streaks of pleasure through me. He gasped as he drew back from me to take a breath. I furrowed my brow and watched as he licked at the threads of saliva that stretched from my cock to his mouth.

"You look so good on your knees for me." My voice a low rumble, my throat constricted.

"Yes, Sir."

His words snapped something in me. My hand shot out and grabbed his hair. He gasped but kept his mouth wide open for me and his eyes on mine.

"Tell me you want it," I muttered, squeezing my fingers to tighten my grip in his hair.

"I want your cock in my mouth." The slight whine in his voice almost buckled my knees.

Tilting my hips, I eased back into his mouth. He hollowed his cheeks and rolled his tongue around me. Each time he swallowed, the pressure around my shaft increased until I was overcome with the sensation.

"Shit, Barden. You're going to make me come."

His answering moan and quickening pace spurred me on. His eyes stayed fixed on mine, his fingers digging into my hips, as he held me close. I growled through gritted teeth as I felt my climax grow.

"Ah. I'm going to... It's coming...Barden!"

Mistress is watching.

Let her see my passion.

He slammed my cock to the back of his throat as my climax exploded from me, my seed pouring into him. My hand tightened in his hair as I cried out, my hips bucking against him. His breath came in heavy puffs through his nose, but his fixed grip and hard suction against my cock didn't release. Wave after wave of prickling heat flowed through me as my climax shook my body. Squeezing my eyes shut, I gritted my teeth as my cock bobbed in Barden's mouth, emptying the last of my seed.

Barden slowly slid his head away from me, easing me out of his mouth, making me twitch when he planted a kiss on my swollen head. I looked down to see him licking a trickle that had escaped his mouth, all the while grinning at me.

"Barden," I whispered in my post-climax haze.

"Mmm, yeah."

"Fuck, Barden," I groaned again.

"Keep saying my name like that, gorgeous, and I'll have to swallow you again."

I grinned, slumping against the wall.

"Down boy," I laughed.

"Rook! Don't do that," he groaned. "Evan speaks to me that way, and it gets me hard every time."

"I'll remember that," I chuckled, winking at him.

"Seriously, Rook!" he laughed. "Don't wink at me like that and expect me to keep my hands off you."

He lunged forward and swiftly licked the head of my cock while still laughing. Twisting out of reach and groaning from the jolt through my now overly sensitive cock, I grabbed Barden's shoulders and pushed him down to the ground, swinging my leg over his waist and sitting on his hips. I stuffed myself back in my breeches.

"Oh, I like this." A broad smile spread over his face as he reached up to rest his hands under his head while I laced up my breeches. "Let's see where this goes."

Reaching down to take hold of his wrists in each of my hands and bringing my face to his, I smirked and replied, "You have had enough for today, greedy boy," before planting a swift, gentle kiss on his forehead.

"Goddammit, Rook!" he whined, bucking his hips up against me.

I held his hands firm, keeping my weight on his hips and enjoyed the view of him wriggling underneath me. We were of similar height but his slim frame didn't stand a chance against my more muscular build. He looked delicious with a pink tinge to his cheeks and an imploring look on his face. A rumble vibrated through my chest, and a feeling of possession washed over me as I held him firmly in my grasp. Barden stilled, his breath shallow.

"You're mine, boy," I muttered, kissing him on the lips this time.

"Yes," he gasped, breathing heavily. "Yes, Sir."

Chapter 29
Rook

Grace arrived in the paddock as I hastily knotted the laces of my breeches. She offered Barden one of the peaches she had brought with her and giggled when he replied, "No thanks, sweetie. I've eaten." While staring directly at me.

Surprised, I spat out the piece of peach I had just bitten off and dribbled the juice down my chin. Grinning, he winked and left.

"It didn't look like you had any breakfast so thought I'd bring you something."

"Thanks," I replied, wiping my sleeve over my mouth.

"So you and Barden are... getting along." She puckered her lips and raised her eyebrows at me.

"Don't look at me like that," I laughed.

"You're totally smitten aren't you?" Her wide smile was infectious.

You know you are grinning like a fool, right?

"Ok, ok." I said, backing away from her, hands held up against any more questions. "I'm done turning the end bed so thought I'd look in on the horses."

The look she gave me told me we were not done with this conversation but I had escaped for now.

The barn was warm and flecks of straw floated in the fading shafts of sunlight coming through the open doors. The herd were dotted about in varying stages of sleep. Seidon was lying down near the fence and lazily turned his head to me as I came towards him. I stilled, hoping not to startle him enough to make him get up. When he nickered softly to me and closed his eyes again, I slowly moved to the fence and reached through to stroke his neck.

"Well now, little friend. You trust me enough not to get up, huh?" His neck was warm, he had clearly been lying in the sun for a while. "Been having a lazy day it seems," I chuckled, gently running my fingers through the tangles in his mane.

His eyes remained closed as I worked my way down his neck and my happiness grew the longer he stayed there, clearly feeling safe in my company despite his prone position. A gentle snore confirmed this and I had to stifle a laugh so as not to wake him.

"I hadn't planned on staying long, little friend, but if you are trusting me to watch over you while you sleep then you are not leaving me much choice."

Settling down against the fence and resting my cheek against my outstretched arm, I closed my eyes, breathing in Seidon's dusty smell and enjoying the gentle sound of his breath as I toyed with a lock of his mane.

Who needs a bed when you have a soft pony to hug while you snooze?

I wonder if Gerard would mind me sleeping in the barn from time to time? The hayloft would be a cosy place to set up a bedroll for the night.

One of the other horses nickered, followed by another, rousing me and I opened my eyes to scan the herd to see what had caught their attention.

"Sorry to disturb you, darling. The horses gave me away."

"Mistress," I mumbled, still half asleep from my impromptu nap. "I didn't know you were here."

"I saw you come this way but didn't want to interrupt your time with Seidon." Tucking her legs under herself, and scooping the skirt of her dress aside, she settled down in the dirt beside me.

She was a wonder. Enchantress of Marieena, bringer of new life, Mistress to us all; and yet she will happily sit beside me, on the dirty barn floor in her silk dress, to share the company of the horses.

Could she be any more perfect?

"I know how precious time is that is spent in their company," she said, slowly offering a hand to Seidon which he gently reached for and rubbed with his nose. "They are a comforting presence when the world feels as though it is falling apart."

A familiar sadness passed over her face.

How I wish I could be more for you.

The sadness was replaced with amusement when Seidon lifted his nose in the air, curling back his lip as if in a smile.

"He's a handsome fellow," she laughed.

"He is. Quick learner and trusting too. In a couple of years, he is going to make a solid riding pony. I look forward to the adventures we will have together."

The Enchantress' face notably brightened at my words. "You imagine spending that time with him, here, and having the honour of being his first rider?"

Realising the presumption of my words, I stumbled over how to respectfully correct myself, "Well, I... hoped... only with your permission, Mistress. That is, I imagined I would... if I could, it would make me happy to be here... for that time, and be the one, yes."

"I look forward to hearing your updates on his progress," she replied, her smile broadening.

Sit in the sun and talk to you about horses?

Is there a better way to spend warm spring evenings?

Sliding closer to her, I rested my hand over hers.

"Since you will be staying with us," she said, her eyes flicking between mine. "It would please me if you would join us for the next new moon ceremony."

"Really?" I asked, taken aback by her invitation.

"You have worked hard, Rook," she replied. "You have made clear your devotion and commitment, and have earned your place at the ceremony."

Overcome, I didn't know how to thank her and opened and closed my mouth several times attempting to convey my thoughts. She smiled kindly and stroked my arm. "It will be my pleasure to have you there, my darling. There is no need to thank me."

"Mistress," I whispered, taking her hand in mine and lifting it to my lips, kissing her palm. Wanting to hold her as long as I could, I ran my fingertips up and down her arm, kissing her palm over and over, enjoying the taste of her.

"Join me in my chamber after supper, my love. I have further use of your lips."

Chapter 30

Rook

Apprehension at the prospect of another evening spent with my Mistress tightened my chest as I made my way to her chamber that evening.

Your offerings serve her, support her, and show your love for her.

This is what you can do to help, even if you aren't her mate.

Serve your Mistress.

Pausing at the door, I took a deep breath before knocking. Evan answered the door. With a broad smile, he beckoned me inside.

"Good evening, Rook, my precious," purred the Enchantress.

She was seated on the sofa with a naked Barden at her side. His legs were splayed around her, wide apart, giving her room to stroke and cup his balls. She teased him while avoiding his bobbing cock, while Barden gently kissed her neck. He tilted his eyes to me and grinned without stopping his loving ministrations.

"Good evening, Mistress," I replied, my eyes darted between her and Barden.

"Remove your clothing and come and sit next to me," she said.

She patted the seat beside her, and I hastened to obey so I could be next to her, eager as ever for her closeness. My cock had already begun to stir, and although I felt self-conscious being completely naked in front of Barden and Evan, their gaze did nothing to quieten my growing desire for whatever my Mistress wanted of me.

Barden slid from the sofa and seated himself at the Enchantress' feet and kissed her legs while I took my place next to her and Evan seated himself on her other side. She reached her arm out to me, and slowly, ran her thumb over my lips, gently parting them, and slipped her thumb into my mouth. Her skin was sweet like honey. Taking her arm in both hands and caressing it, I ran my tongue around her thumb, wanting as much of her sweetness as she would allow me.

"Suck on it, precious," came her firm tone, her green eyes boring into me.

Heat pulsed through my thighs at her words, and I immediately obeyed, making long deep strokes along her thumb, taking as much as I could into my mouth and then running my lips right to the tip. Closing my eyes, I thought of nothing but making my Mistress happy. Her deep sigh drew my eyes to her face, so I could see her response to my affection.

"Keep going, my darling. Show Barden and Evan how much you love your Mistress," she crooned, her other hand still stroked Barden's hair, while Evan kissed her shoulder.

Barden and Evan glanced up from what they were doing to watch me suck on the Enchantress' thumb.

"Oh my," giggled Barden, staring at me, mouth hanging open. "Maybe we should switch places next time we are alone in the paddock, Rook."

Images of our time in the paddock flashed through my mind as I remembered the sensations as Barden swallowed me. Barden's eyes noted the twitch of my cock and smiled.

"I should like to see that very much," the Enchantress said, her eyes sliding between us.

Barden eyed me eagerly.

Desire flared in me at the thought of being on my knees for Barden, hearing him moan for me.

And you know how she likes to watch.

"Yes, Mistress."

Barden jumped to his feet and stood before me, running his hand through my hair. He leaned forward and kissed me. "I only want this if you do," he whispered.

Nodding, I replied, "I do, I do. I just... haven't done it before."

"Any touch you give me will be a pleasure," he replied.

Warmed by his sweet words, I kissed him, long and slow, savouring his taste.

"Open up, handsome," he whispered, straightening, his usual lustful grin returned.

Leaning slowly forward, I licked the swollen head Barden presented to me. He took a sharp breath in, and when I glanced up, I saw his head was thrown back while steady grunts, matching my tongue strokes, escaped his open mouth, accompanied by Mistress' gentle moans as she watched.

He's enjoying it, they both are.

The muscles in Barden's toned stomach spasmed each time my tongue made contact. His soft hand gently cupped my face, fingertips under my jaw, feeling the movement of my throat as I lapped at him.

"You taste good, boy," I muttered to him, my lips pressed against him.

"Ahh, Rook." He huffed out a loud breathy moan, his eyes half closed.

Eager to hear him moan my name some more, and knowing my Mistress had her eyes fixed on me, I opened my mouth wider and slid as much of him in as I could. He let out a sharp groan and planted a hand on my shoulder to steady himself.

The Enchantress slid forward to bring her face closer to mine. "Keep going, my precious, but open your eyes and look at me," she said.

I inclined my head as best as I could with Barden's cock in my mouth so I could look at my Mistress. I was thrilled to see how delighted she looked and increased my pace.

"So eager to please, such a good boy," she said, reaching forward and taking hold of my now firm erection. Surprised by the sudden contact, my hips bucked.

"Move your hips and use my hand to please yourself," she purred, eagerly glancing between my face and my thighs.

Putting my hands on the edge of the sofa and trying to maintain my pace on Barden, I thrust my hips back and forth, sliding my cock through the Enchantress' silky hands. I gasped as fluid leaked from Barden, and as he swelled I struggled not to gag on him.

"I would not see you spill your seed yet, Barden," said the Enchantress. "Evan is eager for you."

"Of course, Mistress," Barden groaned, slowly sliding from my lips and leaning down to kiss me. He lingered, pressing hard against me. He paused a moment, forehead to mine. The swirl of blue marble in his eyes churned like rapid water as he held my gaze.

What is it about you?

You aren't like other men.

Barden's expression faltered a moment before he pressed his lips to mine once more before turning away. Evan stood, sliding his hand to the back of Barden's neck to kiss him before pushing him down to sit on the sofa. Barden moved his hips to the very edge and, raising his legs, slipped his hands behind his knees.

"Beautiful," Evan muttered as he licked his hand and rubbed his saliva along his massive shaft before manoeuvring himself over Barden. Guessing what was about to happen, my face burned, but I was too mesmerised to look away.

The Enchantress slid off the sofa, moved in front of me and, putting her hands between my knees, opened my legs. Sliding slowly forward and wrapping her hands around me, she leaned in to kiss the tip then looked over to Evan and Barden and I did the same.

Evan guided himself towards Barden and slowly disappeared inside him. Barden bit his lower lip, holding his breath, then let out a long sigh as, inch by inch, the full length of Evan's thick cock slid inside him. Evan paused for a moment and let out a deep groan before setting a steady rhythm with his hips. The Enchantress matched the rhythm with her hands on me. I struggled to keep my eyes open as wave after wave of pleasure burned through me.

Evan's pace increased, and Barden grabbed his own cock to pleasure himself. I couldn't keep my hips or my eyes still. I wanted to watch the Enchantress stroking me but was so intrigued and aroused watching Evan and Barden coupling.

"Mistress," I panted.

As Evan's pace increased again, his face turned a darker shade of pink and Barden's breath came in gasps in time with Evan's thrusts. The Enchantress continued to match their pace with her hands which, coupled with the men grunting beside me, pushed me to my climax.

Barden was the first to come.

"Evan!" he yelled, his eyes squeezed shut as his seed spilled over his stomach.

Evan threw his head back and let out a long, low continuous moan while his hips popped and jerked as he came inside Barden. Seeing this and feeling their pleasure, I pleaded with my Mistress. "Mistress!" I grunted, imploring her with my gaze.

"Yes, my darling, give your Mistress her offering now."

Crying out, my seed covered her hands, which continued to move, teasing every last drop out of me.

"An offering fit for the Gods," she purred as I spilt the last of my ejaculation.

"Anything for you, Mistress." I lay back, utterly spent.

I looked over to see Evan collapse over Barden, gently kissing him.

Chapter 31
Rook

Another glorious sunrise creeping through the window greeted me as I opened my eyes the following morning, still curled up in the furs that made up the nest that was the Enchantress's bed.

The pleasures I continued to experience here challenged what I had previously considered to be the definition of love. I was beginning to see that love is as unique as the person you share that feeling with. I was growing to love all that I had come to know here and feel a bond with them that was strengthened by our intimate time together.

The intimacy I had experienced here was so raw. No one hid themselves but instead gave themselves wholly and entirely. Such close familiarity with them in their moments of intense pleasure where they were laid bare gave me a view into who they truly were, which gave me a happiness I hadn't experienced before.

I could have lain in the furs that smelt of my Mistress forever, but I knew it was an important day and one that I was eager to participate in. I arrived in the kitchen to find the room full of people. Gerard served food to the tables while Grace handed out plates, and Tristan brought jugs of water. Evan sat at the head of one of the tables with Bardon next to him. They were deep in conversation when Evan spotted me and waved me over.

"So, today is the day of the new moon, so we are heading out to the forest shrine," he said. "Try not to feel nervous. You have been chosen to come along with us so our Mistress believes you to be ready. We'll all be there, but I have asked Grace and Gerard to take care of you so stay close to them when we get to the shrine. Just do as they do."

I nodded, but I was feeling nervous. I couldn't help it.

Without her Alpha and the belief of the people of Marieena, we have to protect our Mistress. It makes these ceremonies and our offerings all the more important because we are all she has.

Everyone enjoyed a hasty breakfast before Evan called out across the table. "All right, everyone. Time to get going."

Gerard stepped up next to me and wrapping an arm around my shoulder. Grace appeared on my other side taking my hand. "Stick with me," she whispered with a sweet smile. "I'll take care of you." She was practically bouncing on the spot with excitement.

"Thank you," I replied with a smile.

As a group, we headed out of the kitchen into the meadow, which was quiet save for the gentle din of giggling and chattering from the group. The sun hadn't quite risen yet, and the dew still clung to the grass. The cool moisture felt pleasant on my bare feet and I smiled to be in good company and enjoying this beautiful place. Glancing around the group, it was pleasing to see all their beautiful, content faces. They were clearly happy being here and were gladly serving our radiant Mistress in whatever capacity she asked of them. It took me a moment to realise that I was one of their number; happy in my duty and more than willing to be and do whatever our Mistress asked of me to bring her pleasure and joy.

Grace released my hand squealing as Brianna suddenly started chasing her. Catching up to her she wrestled Grace to the floor. They rolled around in the long grass in a mock battle to see who would gain the top position, laughing as they went. They soaked themselves as they kept toppling over each other in the long grass and the wrestling soon turned to kissing, Brianna's hips high in the air, having won. Brianna pinned Grace's hands above her head, holding tight to her wrists while she planted gentle kisses on her face and lips, moving away after each one. Grace frowned and let out small whining sounds as Brianna moved away, and lifted her head in an attempt to maintain contact. This made Brianna smile and continue her torment. It was amusing to watch.

Barden snuck up behind Brianna and spanked her hard on the ass, the contact hard enough to make a sound, then ran off laughing. Brianna shrieked and chased after him, jumping onto his back when she caught him, taking his ear in her teeth and growling. Barden, still laughing, hooked her legs with his arms and carried on walking. I laughed along with them.

Evan and Gerard clearly did a good job of keeping the council's concerns to themselves to spare the younger members of the household the weighty concerns. Let them be content in their duty to their Mistress and lift the mood of the castle with their happiness.

Gerard reached down and helped Grace up. He smiled at her, kissed her then took hold of her hand so they could walk together. Grace held out her hand to me as they approached and leaned in to kiss me, smiling against my lips, brushing the back of her hand along my thigh.

I wouldn't want to see her sweet face marred with concern.

Evan led us through the archway in the courtyard and out into the forest beyond. The sun coming through the trees lit the path ahead. The forest was quiet and cool this early in the morning, and the chatter died away as we entered the forest as if everyone wanted to take in the majesty of the trees. Gripping Grace's hand and relying on her guidance, I closed my eyes and breathed deeply to take in the rich smell. With my eyes closed, I could more fully appreciate the sounds around me; the gentle footfalls of everyone passing over the soft, mossy floor, the birds just beginning their gentle morning chorus in the canopy above, and Grace's soft breaths beside me.

My sense of the unseen became more sensitive, the air itself becoming tangible to me. There was no breeze to rustle through the leaves, yet my skin was aware of something touching it. A pleasant touch wrapped around my body, gently cradling me in sensation that raised the hair all over my body.

Bubbling water added its pretty gurgling notes to the gentle orchestra of the forest and I opened my eyes to see where we were. The mound of the forest shrine, with its arched doorway and the stream that flowed beside it, came into view.

Stopping, Evan stood at the entrance to the mound, as if waiting for something to happen. I looked over at Grace, but she put her finger to her lips and smiled.

The Enchantress emerged from the archway, her hair laced with white flowers and wearing a long white dress in the most delicate of silk. Its thin straps and deep neckline exposed much of her pearlescent skin. Her bare toes were just visible from under the hem. She paused a moment, smiling at each of us before she turned and headed back down the passageway into the mound.

This is it.

The ceremony that our Mistress performs at each moon is about to begin, and I am here to witness it.

The magic I had revered my entire life was to be performed in this very shrine, in mere moments. I would witness our Mistress, the Enchantress of Marieena, gift her magic to us all.

Sweat broke out over my body. I wasn't sure what would happen next or what I should do. I was starting to regret eating breakfast.

For the love of all the Gods, don't mess this up!

I held tight to Grace's hand, and she stroked my arm reassuringly as she went through the archway ahead of me. The floor sloped gently downwards, the sound of bubbling water growing louder as we descended. At the end of the short passageway, the tunnel opened out into a large room. The walls and floor of the chamber looked to be made of large blocks of rough-cut opal, glowing white and glittering with tiny flecks of silver, green and pink, making the chamber shine despite no obvious source of light. There was a shallow pool in the centre of the chamber where the water gently bubbled as though there were a spring beneath, before flowing along a channel built into the floor and out through the wall. Taking stock of roughly the direction the channel pointed, I guessed that this spring was the source of the stream outside.

The Enchantress stood facing the pool, the water glittering as if the sun shone upon it. Everyone moved to form a circle around the edge of the pool.

Grace and I had been near the back of the group, so we were among the last people to take our place in the circle. Gerard held his hand out to me as I approached and gave me a reassuring smile as I took it.

Our Mistress stood, gazing down into the pool, looking in every way a goddess bathed as she was in the pool's light. After a moment of stillness, she stepped into the water and slowly waded to the pool's centre. The water came up to her ankles and soaked the bottom of her dress.

Still holding my hand, Grace moved towards the gap that the Enchantress had created in the circle as Evan did the same on the other side. They joined hands and everyone else in the group followed their example, creating a solid circle with us all looking down on the Enchantress.

Hell, this is it.

Just do what everyone else does.

Silence hung over the chamber, the gentle bubble of the water and the shallow breath of everyone, full of anticipation, the only sounds. I remained silent as everyone else did and waited.

In the pool, the Enchantress slowly lifted her arms and began to sway, her movements gentle, graceful, and hypnotic. As she moved, a voice sounded, high-pitched and quietly spreading around the room. As her body convulsed and her arms flowed around her, I realised the eerie tones were coming from her. I was mesmerised. I could almost feel her fluid movements through my own body as her voice filled my head, sending ripples of pleasure through me.

Her movements became bigger and more powerful. She arched her back and scooped her head back, her silver hair brushing the water's surface as her hands glided over her body.

My body responded to the gasps that fell from her as she took a breath between each note, tightening my chest and hollowing my stomach.

As if in response to her movement, the water around her bubbled more vigorously and soaked more of her dress, which clung to her. The light within the water shined brighter, illuminating her. It created shadows across her features, making her face flicker from ethereal to frightening and back again within seconds.

Grace squeezed my hand, and I looked at her. She was panting, her nipples hard under her tunic and her expression one of unbridled lust. I cast my eyes around the circle to see the others. Brianna was staring intently at the Enchantress, sweat gleaming on her neck and chest. Evan had an enormous bulge in the front of his breeches and was sucking on one of Barden's fingers. Barden was biting his lip and slowly grinding his hips. Gerard and Tristan were kissing, their grip on each other's hand hard enough to turn their knuckles white. Seeing such passion burning through all of them fueled my own.

The Enchantress slid her hands under the straps of the dress, and it slipped down her body and fell into the water. Sounds of delight and appreciation echoed around the chamber. I was overtaken by her; her voice, her movements, her light. Her body shone and shuddered as her hands ran over her slick skin. She squeezed her full breasts and pushed them together, then let them fall as she slid her hands around her throat. My self-control began to waver. An ache gripped my body that pulled me to her, my breath coming out in groans and grunts. Beads of sweat trickled down my body as I fought to do as everyone else did and stay in the circle while every urge in my body was to break away from them and wrap my arms around my Mistress and rub my body against her.

She slid her hands over her smooth stomach, sinking to her knees as she did. Both her hands slipped between her legs and her sweet scent filled the air. She thrust her hips back and forth, riding her fingers, groaning, breasts heaving as her breath quickened, her mouth open as her voice swelled.

It took every ounce of what willpower remained in my addled mind to stay where I was as I watched her touch herself. The rest of the room was a din of moans from the others, but my eyes were firmly on my Mistress. I didn't know how much longer my cock could stay trapped inside my breeches as my hips began to grind in the air to the same rhythm as the Enchantress, and I imagined it was my body, tense and leaking, that she was rubbing herself against.

My hips matched the quickening pace of my Mistress, and as her moaning became louder, her eyes flew open and locked onto mine. The intensity of her gaze hit me as though something had collided with my body. Her fierce eyes blazed, and she screamed her release. My orgasm reached its peak as her body convulsed, and squeezing my eyes shut, my seed exploded from me, coating the inside of my breeches. All around me, I heard the sounds of pleasure, groaning and growling, but it was her voice that rang in my head above all the others.

My whole body shook with my climax. My back arched as a burning sensation flashed down my spine and my legs trembled. I held tight to Grace and Gerard's sweaty hands as I tried to keep myself upright.

What is happening?!

I can barely stand.

When the fire of my orgasm began to fade, I opened my eyes to look at my Mistress. Her movements had slowed, her body relaxing, her hips sinking down into the water. As my breath came easier and I became more aware of my surroundings again, I noticed the pool water had begun to glow golden and rippled more slowly. It seemed to have become thicker, more like the consistency of molten gold than water. The Enchantress still had one hand between her legs, but with the other, she lazily stroked her fingers along the surface of the pool with a serene look on her face as the golden water travelled along the channel in the floor and out through the chamber wall.

She sighed, opened her eyes again, and looked at me. The full pleasure of my orgasm hit me again, and I fell to my knees, shaking.

Fuck!

Get up!

Keeping hold of Gerard's and Grace's hands to steady myself, I lifted my head to look at the Enchantress again, willing myself to stand. With her eyes still fixed on mine, shining gold in the reflection of the pool, she crawled through the water towards me, her eyes burning their dazzling emerald green. The thicker water clung to her, glazing her body in a layer of gold.

She was magnificent.

Climbing over the edge of the pool, she grabbed my face with her hands, splashing it with water droplets, and brought her lips forcefully against mine. Her tongue pushed into my mouth with such ferocity I could hold myself back no longer. Ripping my hands from Grace and Gerard's grip, I wrapped my arms around her, grabbing her hips, digging my fingers into her skin, and pulling her to me. My mind was wild and frenzied, consumed by her in utter delirium. My hips ground into her, my painfully erect cock struggling against my breeches as I rubbed myself against her, breathing in her scent, my nostrils flared, wanting every bit of her I could have. Before I realised what was happening, my hips were grinding more rapidly, and I was climaxing again. Squeezing her tighter, my head flew back as I was blinded by my pleasure. I cried out a long, deep growl that didn't sound like my voice as it rang out around the chamber and reverberated off the walls.

My passion spent, slick inside my breeches, I slumped against her, forehead to her chest, my eyes shut, breathing hard. She gently stroked my hair while the tension in my body eased. Slowly, the sounds in the chamber began to register in my mind again; the bubbling water, the murmur of the others

The Enchantress slid her hands up to my face and tilted my head back so she could look into my eyes, half-closed in my dreamy haze. Her soft eyes gazed deep into mine, her brow furrowed.

I tried to focus my mind and fight the weight that was coming over my body so I could look at her but as I felt the world tilt, I fell into darkness.

I felt my Mistress loosen from my grip and my entire being protested.

Wait, don't go!

Her hand glided over my cheek, leaving a trail of sensation as she left. A knot in my stomach implored me to go after her, but the darkness still held me and try as I might to reach for her, my body wouldn't respond to my commands.

Someone took hold of my arm and put it around their neck as someone else did the same on my other side. They stood me up and carried my limp form.

What's going on?

Leave me be.

Just bring her back.

"...never looked like that."

"... collapsed before"

A sudden blaze of light through my eyelids told me I had been taken outside, but I felt no more until my body was lowered onto something soft.

"In here, he will be safe and close to Mother Earth while he recovers."

Mistress' voice was the last thing I heard.

Strange dreams swirled around my mind. I could smell the earth, rich, strong, and warm beneath me. I dragged my fingers through the soft loam, interlacing myself with the ground. Reaching down deep into the soil, I felt the forest all around me, strong and protective.

I felt it all and felt safe.

In my dreams, I saw my Mistress. Her blurry but beautiful face, full of care and love. Her gentle voice told me all would be well.

The heavy smell of dry wood cocooned me. The soft song of the birds cooing above was a gentle invasion of my haze. The insects carefully made a path around me, their tiny feet scratching against the ground. My eyes were clouded, but I could make out the sun through the leaves above, but all too swiftly, it turned to darkness again. Over and over, this happened until I had no idea how much time had passed.

The nourishing touch of cool and refreshing water invigorated me, rousing me from my peculiar visions.

My sight cleared. The darkness surrounding me had a knotted, woven pattern to it that stretched above me. Blinking hard, I reached my hand up to rub my eyes only to find my hands covered in soil. I gazed at them, confused.

Why am I dirty?

I tried to make sense of the warmth against my back, the textured walls around me, and the light above. Pushing myself slowly up, I ran my hand through my hair, pine needles and dirt fell out of it as I scrubbed my hand over my head. Once upright, I could take in my surroundings more clearly and realisation dawned; the tree hollow I was nestled in was full of dry, dead pines, banked up around my body like a nest, their rich woody smell covering me where some still clung to my skin.

The opening in the trunk of the tree ahead showed a faint light that drew me outside. Crawling into the open air, I eased myself up to standing. My body ached. Every muscle was tight and hard.

My dull mind took some time to register the space around me and recognise the forest I stood in. The stones to my side, smooth and grey, were familiar to me, but I couldn't place them in my memories.

The sound of water pulled me forward as I suddenly realised how thirsty I was. Beyond the stones, a trickle turned into a small stream that I crouched beside and plunged my face into, taking huge gulps of the sweet, refreshing water.

Having drunk my fill, I looked around. Clarity gently unfolded my mind as I recognised the tree I had been nesting in to be the huge old pine tree that stood beside the stone archway that made up the forest shrine entrance.

That means... that path should take me home.

How long it took me to reach the castle, I cannot say. I walked through the forest as though I had drunk one too many cups of mead, slowly stumbling and meandering my way along the path, bumping into trees and scratching myself on bushes as I navigated my way through.

"Rook! Rook!"

A distant voice pierced the fog in my mind and I looked up to see Gerard jogging towards me, the castle wall to his back.

"Hey there, boy. Let me help you." His voice was thick with concern as he took my arm, wrapping it around his neck.

"Let's get you something to eat."

Putting up no resistance, I allowed him to part lead, part carry me to the kitchen, where he gently lowered me into a chair and began pressing small pieces of meat and bread to my lips. Famished, I gratefully chewed them down, eyes closed and my body slumped in the chair.

"We were starting to worry about you, ma' boy. Let's get this down you, and then I'll help you wash all that soil off"

In my haze, the hot, sweet-smelling water of the bath felt good against my grimy skin. Gerard used a soft cloth in slow, deliberate strokes to gently clean all the dirt and foliage stuck to my body.

A full belly and clean skin left me feeling warm and cosy as Gerard dressed me in fresh clothes and guided me through the castle.

"Lay your head down here, boy. Rest now."

Within moments, I had descended into sleep.

Chapter 33
Enchantress

T he ceremonies always produce an intense wave of devotion from those who join me, but the brightness with which this man burns, it's almost too much.

I didn't need to look at him to see his passion shining. His light was the sun on my closed eyelids, intense, blinding, and full of warmth.

Desire, hot and heavy, prickles my skin like nothing I have ever felt before but I must make sure he is well.

He sleeps. He breathes. He will wake up.

Something strange rolls inside me. I push it down.

I must make sure he is ok.

He will be ok.

He will wake.

He has to.

I sing to comfort him.

Chapter 34

Rook

In the darkness, a high-pitched, muffled voice swirled around in my head. It sang of love, new life, and hope.

A shining light came into view, and the voice grew louder as it brightened.

Sitting up, breathing hard, my eyes took a moment to focus before I realised where I was. Confused, I couldn't remember how I had made it up to my room, but that could wait; I could still hear the voice, which compelled me to find its source.

Climbing out of bed and rushing out into the corridor, stumbling as I went, I took the stairs two at a time before blasting through the kitchen and out into the meadow; not thinking, but feeling where I needed to be.

Stepping outside, I found her.

Out in the centre of the meadow, shining in the darkness, was the Enchantress. She stood in profile to me, her beautiful face silhouetted in the moonlight, her hands out to her sides, palms up, utterly naked, showing me her entire body.

Perfection.

Her voice drew me near. It sang of longing and new beginnings.

I strode purposely towards her, needing to take hold of her and not let go.

As she looked at me, her eyes glowed; those wondrous emerald eyes. Her lips parted as she tilted her head back, offering her hand to me in invitation. Reaching her, I dropped to my knees, wrapping my arms around her thighs. I buried my face in her soft hair, squeezing my eyes shut, overcome. Her hair smelled sweet, just like the rest of her. Holding her tight, I drew in deep breaths to fill my body with her; her warmth, her scent, her touch.

"Mistress," I whispered, exhaling against her.

She ran her hand through my hair, eliciting a sigh of pleasure from me and cradling the back of my head as she smiled down at me. Reaching her other hand up, she ran it around the underside of her breast, lifting and squeezing it, leaving dimples in her skin.

My mouth went slack.

Beautiful.

She kneaded the soft flesh, her breast bulging and softening as she moved her hand. Tilting her head down, she ran her tongue slowly over her nipple, leaving a glittering trail. My own tongue moved to mirror hers as I watched her nipple become slick with saliva.

Gliding her hand over her tummy and down between her legs, she cupped her sex and gently rubbed herself. My throat constricted as her hand slid up through her curly hair, a finger remaining between the lips of her sex, running back and forth, disappearing inside her. She watched me watching her.

Pressure on the back of my head pressed me gently towards her. I launched forward and fastened my mouth to her, running my tongue down over her sex and sucked on her sweet flesh. My fingers dug into her hips as I forced her hard against my mouth. Her gasp pulled my eyes up to see her head tilting back as she massaged both breasts, her nipples hard and shining.

I sucked harder on her, running my tongue around and around my mouth to touch as much of her as I could without taking my lips off her. Breathing deeply through my nose, her scent roused me and clouded my senses. I moved my head back and forth and up and down alternately, holding her close to me so she couldn't move away. I wanted to pleasure her, devour her, to hear her scream my name and feel her body shake against me.

Her hips rocked against my mouth and her hand pulled painfully at my hair as she gasped over and over, her voice rising. She looked down at me and I stared into her eyes, barely blinking, wanting to see her in this moment. A flush of pink climbed her tummy and breasts, which shivered and jerked as her hips snapped, jamming her sex against my mouth.

I held tight to her, determined not to lose contact with her.

"Rook!" she gasped, her voice rough and broken.

Grabbing my hair with both hands and holding my head firmly against her, she screamed a long, throaty scream as, with me groaning into her flesh, her warm juices burst into my mouth and trickled down my chin. The strong, sweet scent of her hit the roof of my mouth, choking me.

Holding me there and taking quick breaths, her sex jerked in spasms against my mouth each time I gently ran my tongue inside her. More warm, succulent fluid escaped from her and ran down my chest.

Feeling bathed in her, I reached up to rub her nectar into my chest, relishing it.

She slowly slid her hips away from my mouth, shivering as she did, and bent down to kiss me. Running her tongue over my mouth and between my lips, lapping herself off me. Her hands rested on my thighs, making my skin prickle in response to her touch.

She pushed me gently down to the floor where the grass was soft against my back, tucking her shoulder under my arm and resting her head and hand against my chest. Wrapping my arms around her, I closed my eyes, relishing the feeling of her warm body against mine.

"Rook," she sighed.

"Yes, Mistress." I tilted my neck so I could smell her hair, sweet like honeysuckle.

"My precious, Rook. I see your soul when I look into your innocent eyes," she said. "They betray you any feelings you hold in your heart. Your love blazes so brightly I can bathe myself in its light and feel renewed."

Startled, I felt a lump form in my throat and was suddenly unable to speak. Squeezing her tight to me, a wave of warmth and calm passed over me. I lay, holding my Mistress, content in the knowledge that she knew my heart. This was all I ever wanted. To be here, with her, and have her know the depth of my devotion to her; this magnificent woman who gives every part of herself to see the world bloom.

Chapter 35
Rook

I *'m cold. Why am I cold?*

I groped around the grass beside me to find the space empty. My eyes peeled open and searched the semi-darkness.

She was gone.

Sitting up and rubbing my eyes to clear my sight, I looked around for my Mistress but was disappointed.

The meadow was quiet, the dew on the ground undisturbed. The sky was an inky blue, and faint light from the East told me dawn was only an hour or so away.

A lighted window across the meadow told me someone was already up. I was thankful the meadow didn't have any rabbit holes to fall down in the darkness, as I made my way towards the castle.

Evan was sitting at one of the tables in the kitchen, a pitcher in front of him and a cup gripped in his hands. He looked up at the sound of my feet and smiled. A look of relief passed over his face as his features relaxed.

"Good to see you, lad. How are you feeling?"

"Uh, a little fuzzy-headed, I guess, but ok." Rubbing my eyes with the heel of my hand, I made my way over to him.

He smiled, but it didn't seem to affect his whole face. There was a tightness to his expression that I found curious. Pouring me a cup of water, he gestured to the bench opposite. Falling into the seat, I gratefully accepted the cup, drinking deeply, refilling it several times.

Evan watched me silently, perfectly still, an apprehensive look on his face. Emptying the cup one more time, I raised a questioning eyebrow at him.

"Did Mistress talk to you before she left?" he asked, body rigid but trying to sound casual.

Pausing mid-stretch for the water pitcher, I replied, "What do you mean, before she left?"

"She watched over you while you were in your long sleep but then... left a short while ago."

Apprehension spread through me, and the weight of the water in my stomach suddenly made me feel sick. Dropping my hand to the table, I pushed my cup away from me.

"She left? Where did she go? Hang on... long sleep? What the hell does that mean? Where is she?" Panic threatened to overtake me.

"Keep it cool, Rook. She is well. She has gone into the forest for a while. I don't know when she will return, but she needs some time alone."

"Time alone? Why?! Why did she leave, Evan?!"

A mixture of anger and fear boiled inside me. With my fingers clenched so tight that my nails dug into my palms, my breath coming out in short, sharp pants.

Why would she leave me?

I need her!

I need her!

"Calm down, lad, she's fine. Everything that happened at the last ceremony has been confusing for all of us, but especially for our Mistress. She just needs some time to consider what this all means."

Squeezing my eyes shut and rubbing my fingers over my eyelids in an attempt to calm myself and ease the dull ache that was now pulsing in my head, I tried to string my thoughts into a sentence.

"Ok, I think I am missing something here. What happened? What long sleep are you referring to?" My voice was rough with impatience, exacerbated by the knowledge that my Mistress was not here.

Evan's jaw was clamped. He stared intently at me, a calculating look on his face that I didn't know how to interpret. It wasn't improving my mood and was turning the dull ache in my mind into a sharp stabbing behind my eyes that made them narrow and twitch. Attempting to keep my voice even and only partly succeeding, I continued.

"Evan, what is going on?"

He took a deep breath, closing his eyes for a moment before fixing his gaze on me. "I'm not certain what is happening, but the ceremony at the last moon didn't go... as usual." He paused as if trying to carefully choose his words. "You reacted strongly to Mistress' magic, stronger than either she or I have seen before. She lay you in the great pine, to recover. You have been asleep for near on two weeks."

"Two weeks! How?" The twitch in my eye persisted, as did the pain in my head, which wasn't helped by the fact that I was now clenching my jaw.

"As I said, Rook, I don't know all the details, but after the ceremony, you collapsed," Evan replied. "Mistress laid you in the pine and cared for you while you slept. She came to me to tell me you had woken and asked if I could watch over you while she went into the forest. I'm sure she will have some answers for you when she returns, but I don't know when that will be."

Dumbfounded, I had no reply.

She left...because of me, because of my reaction to her magic.

I messed something up, didn't I?

I knew I would.

I knew I wasn't enough for her.

Anger flooded me at the thought of my idiocy. I had let my Mistress down, and now she couldn't even look at me!

But what about last night?

We were together in the meadow.

Did I dream that?

My head pounded, and my mind was still foggy. Maybe I did dream last night. And now she was alone in the forest.

What if she has realised we... I... am not enough. Not enough to save our dying island. So she has gone to search for her mate.

Gone to search for the one person who can restore her because we... I... can't.

What if she didn't come back?!

Shit.

That thought hit me so hard that my chest heaved, hunching me over the table, my forehead driving hard enough into the wood for it to hurt.

No unworthy fucker who has abandoned her until now is going to take her.

I cannot lose her!

I had to go and find her. I could be pissed at myself later, but right now, I had to go and find my Mistress and convince her that somehow we would find a way to help her.

But what if she doesn't want to be found?

What if she doesn't want to come back?

What if she found happiness settled elsewhere... with him?

My body went slack, heat replaced with a fierce chill as the rage in me was taken over by despair.

What if she... doesn't want to come back?

"Rook! Rook! Hey, Rook," Evan's voice pierced my thoughts. His air of authority seemed to have renewed itself. "Rook! Come back to me, lad. Look at me. Listen to me now. Since the ceremony, the land has bloomed. Everything looks stronger. Mistress will be back, she will. But for now, we are going to carry on as normal, ok?" He raised his eyebrows and fixed me in his gaze. "In the meantime, there are chores to be done, right?"

Evan's sure, pragmatic reassurance was dependable, and though it did nothing to calm me or spread warmth through my despair, his suggestion of busying myself was something that made sense.

The land had bloomed. That means she is well. As long as she is well.

I nodded in reply to Evan, unable to speak.

"Good. There's a tree come down across the Northwest path to the high meadow. Split the wood so we can haul it back, ok?"

Body numb, mind racing, I rose and left.

Chapter 36

Enchantress

What is happening?!

It burns!

Fire, as I have never known.

It burns within me, deep in my core. It swells and rolls in waves that pitch me to the ground.

It spreads through my body, filling me, ravaging me.

Confused, I leave him, curled up asleep in the soft grass and stumble into the forest.

I stagger through the trees, needy with desire, my juices trickling down my thighs.

Touch, contact, friction, something!

My fingers do nothing to soothe the desire. Rubbing against the trees for relief gives none.

I rake my nails over my skin to rid myself of the itch that prickles over my body but I do nothing but bloody myself.

The river, dark and cool, gives me no comfort.

Nothing I do satisfies this need.

Exhausted, I fall and don't get up.

I burrow. Burrow myself into the soil, desperate for contact.

Palms flat on the ground, I call to Mother Earth and ask for guidance.

"Please!" I cry. "What is happening?!"

Intense, blinding, warm light shines in my mind, and a passion burns bright beyond all others.

It's him.

I can feel his body's need for mine.

He's the one my body burns for.

My mate.

Chapter 37
Rook

Focusing on the task at hand and trying not to let my invading thoughts take over, I located the axe in the tool and made my way out into the forest, taking the Northwest path.

Loneliness was something I had not felt in a long time. For most of my life, I had been satisfied in my own company, and while in the Enchantress' castle, loneliness was certainly not a feeling that I had experienced. But now it clawed its way into my body, a savage beast that was not going to leave without a fight... and it was because of her. She was the one who made this place glow and filled our hearts with her fire. The forest was dark and dull despite the sunrise. Nothing glittered, and nothing sang. It seemed everything missed our Mistress... or was the world just dull to me, without her.

Roughly a mile from the castle, my path was barred. The old oak had split through the centre of the trunk and twisted as it had fallen, tearing the bark and splintering the wood, thankfully missing its neighbours and only damaging a small thicket on the opposite side of the path.

The old bark was a pale honey colour, dry and brittle. What was once full of life, both in its own spirit and in those who relied upon it, was now empty and quiet. Pausing a moment in reverence for the loss of something that had lived a selfless life that had spanned way beyond the years of my own, I quietly offered my thanks. It seemed the right and honourable thing to do before taking my axe to it.

The brief interlude in my concern for my Mistress, in which I had taken time to give thanks to the old tree, was indeed brief as my thoughts once again turned to my despair.

Why would she leave without speaking to me?

Having assessed the thinnest part of the broken section, I raised my axe and slammed it into the wood, a hollow sound resonating.

It's all my fault.

I shouldn't have gone to the ceremony.

I wasn't ready!

Heat rose in my chest, so I quickly dislodged the axe head, took a sweeping arc over my shoulder, and slammed it into the tree again.

I was too weak to be in the presence of my Mistress' magic.

I picked up the rhythm with the axe, each time aiming to dislodge the head sooner to keep the rhythm of my swing as I deepened the notch in the wood.

If only I hadn't been so selfish, so eager to see her power.

My shoulders warmed from the effort, perspiration creating a sheen over my skin as swing after swing, I slammed the axe into the dry wood.

She was disappointed with me.

I had let her down, and now the others would suffer her absence too.

My chest heaved at the thought, and ignoring the burning in my hands, I increased my pace.

But, according to Evan, the land was stronger.

Maybe... she left... Because she finally found... him.

My eyes prickled, and I growled at myself, roughly rubbing the back of my hand over them.

Would she come back?

The calluses of my hands began to crack with the relentless pace I set myself.

Would she want to see me again?

Blood stained the axe's wooden handle as the skin of my palms split open.

What if she had... found her mate?

Bile burned my throat, and a roar erupted from deep in my chest.

A sudden pain burst behind my eyes and streaked down my back as though a hot blade had sliced along my spine, twisting at the base. Staggering backwards, I dropped the head of the axe to the ground, leaning on the handle. Gritting my teeth, I looked around for an assailant that wasn't there.

What the fuck!?

I forced the heel of my hand against my head, letting out a cry as another jolt ripped down my spine, immediately arching me backwards. My knees buckled and dropped to the ground, slicing the flesh of my thigh along the sharp head of the axe.

"Gods damn it!"

What the hell is wrong with me!?

Anger flared through me as I watched a thin slice open along the outside of my knee and a dribble of blood emerge. My body trembled; exertion, exhaustion, loneliness... and something else entirely unknown to me.

I just needed her back.

Day after day, my body burned as I drove the axe into the dead tree, working along the length of its trunk, creating chunks small enough to be lifted. I was halfway along the trunk when I finally consented to pause at Gerard's insistence that I allow him to bind my hands to stop my callouses bleeding and reduce the risk of blistering any more of my skin. I agreed to the short respite, but once he was done, I went right on with my task, refusing any offers of help.

Don't think about it.

Just keep doing this.

This is something you can do.

I channelled the anger I felt at myself into the axe, gripping the handle tight as my sweat made it slick.

It's your fault she is gone.

Shut the fuck up!

Growling, I doubled my efforts, my shoulders and back screaming in pain, but I just pushed all the harder. Each time the axe slipped or missed its mark, I cursed at myself, my anger boiling to the surface. More than once, the heat boiled over and, coupled with my frustration, I was unable to hold it in any longer, despite my efforts towards the tree, and a cry would escape me that would ring out around the forest, leaving my throat raw and nothing but despair in my heart.

The forest remained dull around me. No birdsong to brighten my spirits, no gentle rustle of a breeze to give me some inclination that the world continued without her. We were all waiting, waiting in our loneliness for our Mistress.

I didn't go back to the castle. The warm soil of the forest floor made a perfectly adequate bed on mild summer nights, so I slept right there in the forest each night. I didn't want to see anyone, knowing I would be poor company but also having no desire to discuss where my Mistress was. She wasn't here, and that's all there was to it. Sheer exhaustion dropped my body to the ground each night.

I swung my axe until my arms shook, and I couldn't grip the handle any longer, all in an attempt to avoid considering the world without her.

Everyone took turns in coming to leave me parcels of food and skins of water. It was appreciated, and I would give my nod of thanks but make no effort to converse. Gerard had sat on the end of the trunk yet to be chopped and tried to speak to me about Seidon, saying something about my young colt not seeming himself of late and how he would likely enjoy a visit from me. Warmed by his effort to comfort me but in no mood to talk, I thanked him for the water and carried on with my task. Barden had tried his hardest to convince me to go back to the castle to sleep each night so that my body could at least get some decent rest. Shaking my head at his suggestion, I accepted the fresh skin of water he had brought, set it down to one side, and continued with my work.

Several days of hard manual labour followed by nights spent sleeping in the open forest with no one but yourself for company can dampen the hottest anger, even that which is directed at yourself. My blood and sweat had poured from me as I vented my frustration until nothing was left. The moment finally came where pausing in my task, my mind remained free of anger and despair, and in its place, something else appeared.

Maybe if she returns, I can beg her to let me stay.

Just stay and perform my simple duty of farming the land.

I will remain in the castle, I won't go to the shrine, and all will be well.

A small glimmer of hope at that thought lodged in my mind.

If she could just come back and I could stay.

If she could just come back.

Chapter 38

Rook

Finally, the dead tree lay in pieces. It had taken me nearly a week to work my way along the entire length of the thick trunk, but at last, it was done. I had refused all offers of help from the others, knowing that I needed the time alone and the responsibility of something I could do, coupled with the sheer effort to keep my mind off my Mistress.

Gerard hitched two horses to a small trap and, with Evan's help, load after load had been thrown in and stacked back at the castle.

"This will last us a good while." Gerard tried to sound cheerful, but I didn't have the heart to play along.

My mind had finally quietened. I had thrown every possible curse at myself in accusation for my Mistress leaving, and all I had left was the weight of my heavy heart. I teetered on the edge of my anguish, knowing if I gave it too much thought, I would crawl back into the great pine, curl up and refuse to leave for anyone but her.

The midday sun was high and hot as we brought in the trap with the last load of wood. All three of us were soaked in sweat and covered with dirt.

I paused a while to catch my breath, my hands against the empty trap. The not-so-unpleasant smell of sweaty horses filled my nostrils when something shining across the meadow caught my eye. The heat waves blurred my vision, which only allowed me to make out something silver, like a waterfall, gliding across the meadow. I squinted and lifted my hand to shade against the sun, trying to figure out what it was. The form grew more defined as it edged closer, its outline becoming clearer.

It was her.

My breath hitched, my chest tightened, and tears instantly burned my eyes.

She had come back to us.

To me.

A choked laugh tinged with relief fell from me as I tried to draw breath.

The world suddenly blazed with light and colour again. A mighty chorus of bird song erupted from the trees in celebration of her, carried across the meadow by a cheerful breeze that whistled its delight. The ground beneath my feet tingled as if in anticipation of the reunion I had also longed for.

I ran. My exhaustion forgotten, I ran. The air flew past my ears, blocking out any other sound, my eyes fixed on her. She, and nothing else, consumed me. Gone was the loneliness, gone the despair and self-deprecation. She had returned! Nothing was going to keep me from her, and as long as she would allow it, I would hold her and tell her again and again of my love for her.

Reaching her, I wrapped my arms around her waist, lifted her feet off the ground and spun, holding her tight in my arms. A joyous laugh fell to my ears, swelling my heart. Placing her back on her feet, I dropped to my knees to wrap my arms tight around her thighs, burrowed my face into her abdomen, and wept.

I cried into her delicate body, pouring the turmoil, guilt and heartbreak that had threatened to overwhelm me for days. My hoarse voice coughed out my sobs, my tears stained her dress, and my fingers gripped her thighs with no intention of releasing her. I drew ragged breaths, barely able to breathe but enough to take in her smell, her glorious perfume filling me with relief and hope.

Fuck, her scent. Has she always smelled this good?!

She held tight to my shoulders, and when her quiet sobs reached my ears, I slid my face up her dress to look at her. Her sweet face was flushed, eyes glittering with tears. So beautiful.

"My darling, my Rook," she whispered.

Oh, to hear my name from her lips again. It had been agony to be without her for so long.

"Mistress," I croaked, my throat tight and rough. "You came back to me."

"Of course, my beloved, I will always return to you. You are my one."

A warm sensation trickled through my body at her words, my skin tingled, and relief flooded my mind.

"Where did you go? Why did you leave me?"

"Oh darling, I'm so sorry," she replied. "I was concerned about what happened at the last ceremony but didn't want to worry you when I didn't have the answers. Your reaction to my magic was so strong. I went deeper into the forest to better connect with myself and Mother Earth in the hopes of seeing things more clearly."

"And did you? Find the answer. Please say you are staying." I made no effort to hide my desperate tone as I searched her face for any hint of the answer.

Her smile reassured me. "I am staying, my love, and yes, the answer became clear to me." Her manner became suddenly timid. She cast her eyes down, and a flush spread over her cheeks as her expression turned coy, which intrigued me. This manner was unlike her. She was usually so sure and confident in everything, yet she blushed as a maid might. Eager for her to continue, I kept my eyes fixed on her face, waiting for her to confide in me.

Looking back at me, the pink flush still dusting her cheeks, giving her the most beautiful glow, she continued, "Your presence at the last ceremony must have... triggered something in me which my magic responded to. It flooded me in a way I have never experienced before. At each ceremony, the love of those around me builds my passion and causes my magic to filter into the water, but the water doesn't usually change the way it did. It glows but has never turned into the liquid gold form it did when you were present. Your love strengthened my magic the way no other ever has." She paused, her eyes shining with unspilled tears as she cleared her throat, which had wavered for a moment.

"While you slept in the old pine, I could feel something different inside me. Once I knew you were waking from your long sleep, I went out into the forest, and that's when my body suddenly came alive like it never has. A fire burned through me, and I pleaded with the Gods to give me the answers and finally, the truth was made clear."

Swallowing several times as if gathering herself, she went on, "After all this time, after all these years, waiting, hoping, thinking it might never happen, I had my first heat."

She paused, her eyes imploring me to respond, but was met with my confused silence.

"Your...heat?" I finally replied.

I had no idea what she meant by this.

"I was confused and scared at first; I didn't understand," she said. "I'm an ancient; I have seen generations of humans while I have taken care of Marieena. Why now? After days of fire, the longing came, and I realised it was you. You, my darling Rook. You who are compelled to me, you who have yearned for me. It's you that brings on my heat now because you are my one. I wasn't sure my mate would ever come, but there is something about you beyond all others, and my body knows it."

Hardly daring to hope that she meant what I thought she meant and what was the only thought in my mind, I tentatively asked, "I'm... your mate?"

A look of utter love, warmer and truer than I had ever seen on her beautiful face before, shone through the blush that had been there a moment ago. "You are, my love. It is you. There is no doubt in my heart that it is you."

A light, brighter than the sun of all the summers of my life, burst behind my eyes, coursing through me, filling me with an utter elation beyond that which I had ever experienced. Squeezing my arms around her thighs more tightly, I jumped to my feet, lifting her into the air and roaring with such abandon and volume that it echoed through the meadow, disturbing birds in the trees beyond. She wrapped her arms around my neck, pulling my cheek to her breast and laughing as she rubbed her face over my hair.

This was more than I could have ever hoped would be. In my most wild and fantastical dreams, I would never have thought myself worthy of laying claim to this being that I considered beyond the beauty and grace of all others. Yet, here she was, declaring to me that above all the people in the world who adored her, worshipped her, devoted themselves to her, it was my devotion that shone through brighter than all of them, so much so that our very natures had compelled us to each other and would bind us together. Now I would never have to let her go. I could spend the rest of my life gazing upon her beauty and loving her so completely that she would never have cause to doubt it.

My Mistress, my Goddess, my Mate.

Chapter 39

Rook

As my vision widened beyond my Mistress, I noted the others had gathered in the meadow and were slowly approaching to welcome her home. Their steps were tentative until we glanced up and registered their presence. Feeling their need to show their gladness at her return, I took a step back from her, threw my arms wide and declared, "Our Mistress is returned to us!"

A cheer rang out as they hastened to gather around her. Gerard was the first to reach us. "Mistress." The relief in his breathy voice was touching. He knelt before her and gently, taking her hand, pressed it to his lips. The others quickly followed suit, placing their lips upon her hands and arms and expressing their relief and joy that she was among them again.

"My darlings, how I have missed you all!" She beamed at them, stroking their blushed cheeks and running her hand through their hair. "What a joyous day this is to be reunited with you and be in the presence of your love once again."

"We are overjoyed to have you home, Mistress. But please, tell us where you have been. We are eager to know all is well." Evan's eyes flicked between hers, desperately searching.

Of course. I hadn't considered how concerned, in my addled panic, the impact her absence would have on Evan. He had been with her a long time, and though he presented a calm facade for us to lean on, the worry must have all but consumed him.

"Darling Evan, all is more than well. We are to celebrate, for I bring you the news that you are now blessed with not only a Mistress but a Master as well." She cast her eyes on me, pure rapture spreading across her face as tears trickled down her rosy cheeks.

The din that followed blocked out all other sounds. Gerard grabbed me around the waist. "Haha, my boy!" he yelled, while Evan and Barden clapped me across the back, crying out their delight, broad smiles lighting their faces.

Grace and Brianna squealed and hugged their Mistress while Tristan kissed her cheek and said, "Mistress, such a blessing. I'm sure I speak for us all when I say what an utter gift this is."

"Oh, Tristan, I can always rely upon you for your sweet words." Placing a gentle kiss on his lips, she took hold of his hand and rested her head on his shoulder. Seeing them together, all of them, swelled my heart. The love that was shared among them was tangible.

"Mistress, would a bath please you after your journey?" Grace eyed the soil that clung to the Enchantress' hands.

Giggling, she replied, "That would be wonderful, and I want you all to join me." The sultry look that stirred my passion darkened her eyes as her gaze swept the group, pausing on me.

"Come on, stinky dog, let's get you in the bath" Barden giggled, appearing at my side as Gerard grabbed my hand and dragged me forward.

"Hey, you heard Mistress, it's Master now," I laughed, attempting to keep a serious tone in my voice but failing utterly, making Barden laugh all the harder.

"Yes, Sir," he replied, winking at me.

The bathhouse had much raucous energy as everyone eagerly stripped and jumped into the water. I hung back outside with my Mistress so that I could have a moment alone with her. Stepping close to her and sliding my fingers into her hair, I tipped her head back and pressed my lips firmly to hers. Her hands wound around my waist, and she pressed her slender body against mine.

"I have missed you," I sighed.

The swell of her breasts pushing against my chest and her sweet smell ignited my passion and swelled my cock.

"So it seems." We chuckled together, holding each other in silence for a moment, enjoying being close to one another again.

"Tomorrow is the new moon, my love. I want us to seal our union during the ceremony by lying together in the pool to share our offering."

"You want me to join you in the pool?" I asked.

"Of course. You are my mate, and our union will provide a far greater offering of magic than I could provide from my pleasure alone."

Anticipation knotted my stomach at the thought of entering the shrine during the new moon again, the last ceremony still very raw at the forefront of my mind. The concern must have been evident on my face, for a gentle hand slid over my cheek.

"Your place is with me, my darling. I have waited a long time to lie with my mate, and I want it to be marked by the ceremony. You have already proven your worth beyond all others, and now it is the simple matter of our union." Leaning in so I could feel her breath on my ear, she continued, "I am eager to feel you inside me, stretching me, filling me the way no other has before."

A groan rumbled in my chest, and I buried my nose in her neck to plant kisses and gentle nips over her soft skin. Her timid squeaks were so small and quiet, and her demeanour coy, so unlike her, yet she seemed so very happy that it made my body swell. Spurred on, my rumble deepened, and I squeezed her tightly to me, rubbing my stiff shaft against her through her dress.

"Tomorrow, my eager love," she said, "Tomorrow. I want you to be so full with seed that you fill me completely."

Fuuuck.

"I want you so much." My groan turned to a growl at the thought of sliding myself deep inside her and grinding my hips against her until she was brimming with my seed.

Her sharp nails pinching the skin of my waist made me jump and pull back from her to see a mischievous smile spread over her face.

"In the bath, stinky dog," she laughed.

"Yes, Mistress," I replied, laughing with her.

From the sounds coming from the bathhouse, it seemed what had started as a water fight had spiralled into lovemaking, with everyone included. Naked, writhing bodies were spread over the edge of the bath, floor, and surrounding benches. Tristan was on his hands and knees on the floor, with Gerard kneeling behind him, his hips rocking, teasing Tristan with long, slow strokes, while Tristan's mouth was wrapped around Evan's thick shaft. Grace had her mouth wrapped around the bulbous head of Barden's cock, while Brianna stood over him, legs spread while he buried his face in her.

"Welcome home, Mistress," I growled, fixing her with hooded eyes.

Holding my gaze with her blazing eyes, she dragged me into the bathhouse.

Chapter 40
Rook

Following the Enchantress, her silk gown trailing behind her, we descended. There was no concern in me now as I entered the shrine. This was where I was supposed to be. I had found my place, my purpose, my mate.

The circle around the pool was formed, and the room fell silent, all eyes on our Mistress.

She turned to me, eyes smouldering. "Rook, my love. Lie down in the pool."

"Yes, Mistress."

Casting away my clothes, I stepped into the shallow pool and was surprised at how warm the water was. I lay on my back, the pool water lapping at my sides, and looked up at her towering above me. Her body shone in the light of the pool. She stepped into the water, placing a foot on either side of my hips.

A pearlescent shimmer rippled over her skin as the water lapped around her ankles. My eager hands slid up her legs, smooth and warm under my touch. She purred in response, making my cock strain for her.

Slowly, she lowered her body over me, her nipples grazing my abdomen, her eyes locked on mine as she glided up my body and brought her lips to meet mine. A jolt whipped down my spine, and I arched my back up to meet her. Wrapping my arms around her shoulders, I pulled her down to me, squeezing her close.

She slid her wet sex along my rigid shaft, and a groan slipped from my throat in response. Her cheek slid affectionately down my jaw where she paused, continuing the slow grinding of her hips while she rested her lips close enough to my ear for me to feel her breath.

"My magic has been coursing through the water searching for you, and now it has finally brought you to me." Her voice was silk. "Here, in this sacred place, we will seal our bond, connected to the rest of the island by the water that brought you to me."

"I'd have thrown myself in the river long ago if I had known it would have brought me to you," I replied

Her face contorted a moment, eyebrows raised. "Oh, Rook."

The movement of her hips sped up, sliding herself along me, my seed lubricating her movement further. She pressed her soft, sweet lips to mine and lay against me, resting the head of my cock against her opening.

"It's always been you, Mistress," I murmured, keeping my lips against hers, feeling tremors from her flesh against me and heat in the water at my back.

Sliding my hands over her hips, I squeezed her flesh hard enough for her to sigh against me and pushed a fraction of myself inside her but holding her firmly enough that it went no further. I wanted to savour this moment, feeling her deliciously tight sex stretch around me. It took every ounce of my willpower not to push inside her, but I didn't want to hurt her, and I was determined to feel and enjoy every inch of her. The soft murmur of the others around us seemed to register in the heat of her skin. She felt their adoration and glowed all the brighter for it.

"Rook!" A moan escaped her as she grabbed my hair and tried to push herself further down, but my arms tensed, held rigid to keep her where she was. Her muscles clenched around me with such force I had to tilt my hips up to keep the tip of my cock inside her. She whimpered, eager for more, but I relished the anticipation.

"Easy, Mistress. You will have all of me soon enough." I reached up to slide my tongue between her lips. "Listen to them, listen to their appreciation of you." She moaned, pushing her lips hard against mine, and continued to squeeze the tip of my cock, making it hard to keep her still.

At last, I couldn't wait any longer. "Mistress, look at me."

There they are, those eyes.

Her eyes glowed as they never had before; her black pupils blown wide, ringed by two bands, one of her usual emerald green and one within it that was pure light, shining from within her.

Once her eyes were fixed on mine, I slid my entire length inside her. Sensation exploded through my hips as her tight muscles rippled over every inch of me from root to tip. My fingers dug deeper into the flesh at her hips, holding her to me, my teeth gritted, and my eyes squeezed shut at the almost unbearable pleasure ripping through me. Fire flashed through my whole body, sweat beading all over my skin as spasms of heat scorched through my limbs. The pool water began to bubble around us, specks landing on my skin and tingling, adding to the pleasure.

Oh, how much I have wanted this.

To be this close to her.

To be wrapped around and inside her body.

She grazed her teeth along my shoulder to the base of my neck, sending jolts of sensation through me. A deep rumbling built in my chest that escaped my throat as a long, low growl.

We stayed locked together in a tight embrace of clenching muscles and sharp breaths for a few seconds of pure pleasure before she began to rock her hips against me, forcing my cock further inside her, stretching herself around me. With each of her movements, jolt after jolt of pleasure caused my hips to buck against her.

Her tightness, rather than easing as she became slick, seemed to contract and strangle me. With each thrust, a flash of pain shot through my hips. In my haze, I looked down to where our bodies me to see a bulge of flesh appearing at the base of my cock. I watched, eyes blurred in an almost unbearable mixture of pleasure and pain as each time she pushed her hips down onto me, the base of my cock grew more prominent.

What the hell?!

I choked, confused by what I saw but too overwhelmed by the sensation to fully consider what was happening. The Enchantress slowed her movement, concern flashing across her face when she took in my expression. She followed my gaze to where our bodies met.

"Rook!" she gasped, leaning further back to see better where we connected, running her fingers over herself and then me in turn, her delicate touch making me jerk from my sensitivity. "I knew it!" she cried, leaning forward to kiss me. "My heat... our bond... it's your knot!"

"My what!?" I barely registered her words, my mind foggy with desperate need.

"Your knot! Your knot!" Her eyes were wide and her face flushed, "It must be because of my heat. You are... an Alpha."

I couldn't make sense of what she was saying. All I knew was that her body pressed against that swelling felt fucking amazing, and I needed more. Wrapping my arm around her waist, I flipped us, so she was lying in the pool. The water shining around her sent flecks of pearlescent light glittering over her skin.

My Goddess.

Sliding my arms under hers, I wrapped my hands over her shoulders and brought my knees high under her thighs, lifting her hips and opening her sex to me. With an iron grip on her shoulders, I buried my nose into her neck and slammed my hips against hers, my swelling cock pushing hard against her. Wrapping her legs around my waist and clawing at my back, she spurred me on. My mind and senses were full of her and nothing else. My hips moved without thought, faster and harder with each thrust, pushing my swelling harder against her until suddenly, with a slight adjustment of angle, I forced it inside her.

The deep growl that escaped me and her answering scream filled the room, echoing off the walls. I exploded in blinding pleasure. The intense heat filling me took over, and I had urges beyond my own. Compelled, I wound my fingers in the Enchantress' hair, wrenching her head back, and as the intensity reached its peak, I dug my teeth deep into her neck, clamping onto her.

Her soft, slick body bucked beneath me as her pleasure ripped through her. My muscles were rigid and tense as the peak of my orgasm raged through my entire body. I burned from the inside, a familiar streak of near pain shooting down my spine. Sweat ran down my back and dripped from my brow.

I opened my eyes to be blinded by light. Releasing my teeth from the Enchantress' neck, I raised my head to see her body glowing, eyes burning, and the pool around us shone as if the sun itself sat within it; molten gold waves, thick like honey, rippled around us, coating us in a metallic sheen. A recognition beyond my comprehension settled itself deep within me, filling me with a sense of belonging and peace.

It's **her.**

My body pulses for her.

Exists for her.

She lay, arms splayed out to her sides, legs still wrapped around my waist, and her teeth clenched, emitting a low, steady scream.

Squinting down at her, worry shadowed my mind. I hadn't seen her skin glow this way before.

She panted, her body slowly relaxing and going limp, the light around us fading as she settled.

"Rook," she sighed.

"Mistress. Are you OK?"

"My Rook," she reached her hands, covered in the gold of the shrine water, to my cheeks and kissed me, tears staining her face.

"You are the one. The one my magic has been waiting for, the one I have been waiting for." She coughed out a sob. "I didn't think you would ever come. I thought my magic would go on fading, and I would fade with it, deeply alone."

An overwhelming need to protect her burned hot through my body, bristling my hair while a growl issued from deep in my chest. "I will never let that happen. You are mine, and I will love and protect you always."

Resting my body down against hers, I buried my nose deep in the cleft of her neck and inhaled her sweet smell.

Chapter 41
Rook

Contentment and happiness beyond anything I had ever felt before welled within me. I was bonded in every sense to my true love, my mate, my Mistress. We lay bound together, breathing as one.

As I made an experimental adjustment in my weight, with a mind to move, I found that I was unable to. My cock was swollen and wouldn't release from her. I grunted with the strange feeling, half sitting up in a position my cock would allow, and looked down at her, puzzled.

She smiled a knowing smile and giggled. "Darling, it is your knot. It binds us together to hold your seed inside me to seal our bond."

Blinking rapidly, brow furrowed, I took a moment to take in what she had said. As my post-coital haze cleared, more of her words came back to me. "Because I'm an Alpha?" I asked.

Her sweet face gave me a reassuring look. "Yes, my love. You are an Alpha. Your knot is proof of this."

"But how? How is this possible?"

Her legs still wrapped around my waist; she gently pushed me up, my cock still swollen inside her, and encouraged me to sit with my back leaning against the smooth edge of the pool. Having forgotten the others, I was surprised when she beckoned them to come and sit at the pool's edge. "Come, everyone. I want to share this with all of you. This is an extraordinary moment that I never thought would happen, and I want you all to be a part of it."

My face reddened slightly under everyone's eager gaze, but when I looked into their faces, the awe I saw there filled me with such appreciation and love that any pang of embarrassment was short-lived.

She waited for everyone to be seated and comfortable before turning back to me. "The original Alphas sprang to life from the scattered seed of the Sky Father. Wherever the Sky Father's seed landed in open ground, it seeped into the rich, fertile warmth of Mother Earth and from that union came the Alphas."

She paused a moment, watching my face for understanding. Hesitantly, I nodded, and she continued.

"Alphas are few and remain dormant until they meet their mate. Their nature compels them to protect Mother Earth, and their strength has been called upon throughout history to protect the land. In their dormant form, they have mated and bonded with others, including mortals, but innately, they are always loyal to Mother Earth and seek her out beyond all others." Turning to me, she smiled. "You are descended from these original Alphas and, having bonded with me, have come into your true self."

She sighed, a content look on her face. "Mother Earth made me, I am the daughter of a Goddess, and this is what called you to me, what bonded you to me. You were always destined to be mine."

Silence followed her words, the gentle lapping of the pool water the only sound in the chamber. I glanced around at the others to see the shock I felt on their faces.

This can't be right... Can it?

I'm just...

How can I be...

After opening my mouth to say something, realising I didn't know what to say or how to form my question, I closed it again.

Her face was gentle with understanding, as if hearing my thoughts, she replied, "I was there when the original Alphas came into existence. I know what you are. Did you never wonder why your compulsion to be here and devote yourself to me was so strong? Your very nature binds you to me," she whispered.

"What... What does this mean? What do I have to do?"

A broad, warm smile spread across her face. "Just love me, my darling, that's all."

Warmth spread through my body, and I pulled her to me, wrapping my arms around her shoulders and burying my nose in her hair.

Chapter 42

Rook

We exited the shrine to be blinded by a bright light. It burned my eyes, and they needed a few moments to adjust. The Enchantress's gleeful cry drew my attention to her. Her expression was one of pure joy. Following her gaze, I looked out into the forest to see such magnificence. It was as if I was basking in the splendour of the natural world for the first time.

A delicate mist of rain swirled on the breeze, coating everything in tiny diamonds that shone, covering everything in little rainbows. The forest had never looked so bright and full. The leaves of every tree and thicket had taken on a glossy finish, shining as though the stars themselves had come down from the heavens to rest upon them. Bunches of fruit, rich and saturated in colour, were so plentiful the boughs they sat upon dipped under the weight.

The sun shone with a brightness and a warmth that had been equalled by no summer before it and filled my body with such vigour. The forest had never been so alive. Insects, bees, birds and animals; there was movement and sound of activity throughout the trees and the sky above.

The Enchantress squeezed my arm, giving it an excited shake. With a gleeful cry, still naked and covered in the gold water from the shrine pool, ran into the forest, skipping amongst the trees, holding her hands up to the rain, her smile as radiant as the sun.

"I can feel everything!" she cried, "Every flower, every tree, every blade of grass!" She was a gold-spattered nymph, joyous at the renewed strength of the world. She shone, her delight evident on her beautiful face.

Our Mistress danced about the clearing, her voice ringing out in cheerful notes. Tears filled my eyes. The others joined her, dancing a circle around her, calling out and exclaiming their elation. The rain had soaked them, but that just seemed to add to their delight. I looked on, feeling utterly blessed.

Raising my face and palms to the rain, I soaked in the wonder of it all.

Love strengthened the world; love, devotion and the undying need to protect the one being who brought me happiness beyond all others.

Chapter 43
Enchantress

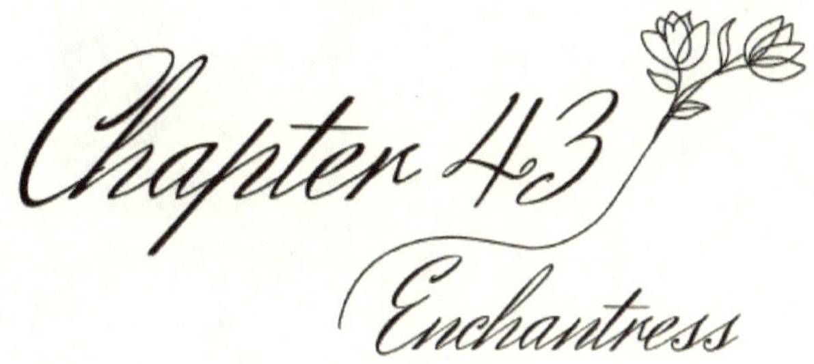

Joy! Elation! Delight!

Rook, an Alpha.

My Alpha.

My Mate.

My sweet, gentle Alpha who renewed the world with love.

Epilogue

“I would have you know my name.”

“Your name, to me, is my love.”

“I would have you know it just the same.”

“You grant me a high honour.”

“The honour would be mine to hear my name on your lips. To others, I am the Enchantress; Mistress of Marieena, Deity of the land, Goddess of love, but to you, my darling Rook, I would have you know me as Deo.”

“Deo.”

The End

Acknowledgments

I have been so lucky to have made some wonderful friends in the writing community and I want to thank you all for your support and friendship. My joy of writing has been bolstered by having you wonderful people to share it with.

To Lyx Robinson; your generosity with your time and expertise has been appreciated beyond what words can express. It has been such a pleasure to spend so much time conversing with you, dear lady. The day will come when I can stand it no longer and will insist on your company in my horse's paddock where we can sit in the sun and chat for hours.

To Niccolite Slater; you boosted my confidence and gave me support time and again, you told me what I needed to hear while being kind and gentle with this baby author. I could not have wished for a more awesome writing partner. Thank you, my friend, thank you a hundred times over.

To Alexis Maree; your support and belief in me, and love of this book, fills me with so much joy. You are a kindred spirit, my sweet, and my days are all the happier having you in them.

To my betas; Mia Fury and Nia Morelle. Your support and hype have meant so much, thank you so much.

To all my ARC readers; Thank you! Your early feedback and comments made me so very happy and they are greatly appreciated.

About the Author

I am a Welsh-born author living in Wales, UK with my husband, children and many fur babies including my beloved horses. A passion for the nature world coupled with a love of romance and writing have fueled this, my first novel, which I sincerely hope you adore as much as I do.

Work has begun on book two of 'The Rook Series.'

For updates, sign up to my newsletter or find me on social media.

www.ingramcontent.com/pod-product-compliance
Lightning Source LLC
Chambersburg PA
CBHW061807190726
48289CB00007B/2099